THE NEON
GRAVEYARD

GEORGE BAXT

THE NEON
GRAVEYARD

GEORGE BAXT

ST. MARTIN'S PRESS
NEW YORK

Library of Congress Cataloging in Publication Data

Baxt, George.
The neon graveyard.

I. Title.
PZ4.B35456Ne   [PS3552.A85]   813'.5'4   79-16429
ISBN 0-312-56412-0

This book is for
Steven Dansky and Bret Adams
and special guest star,
Leonard Soloway

1

Young man, I think you've had it.

It was the first time he admitted defeat to himself. It was the first time he'd ever felt this tired, this beaten, this bloodied. He leaned against the grillwork door gasping for breath, wondering what to do next. His right eye was painfully swollen, and the left one was curtained with blood oozing from his lacerated eyebrow. He leaned forward and shook his head and saw drops of blood dapple the flagstones at his feet. The fierce wind blowing at this height did everything but scatter the confusion in his mind. His thought processes were becoming as unreliable as a fair-weather friend. He knew he had been doped.

He could feel the dampness of the fog rolling in from the Pacific and wished someone had the decency to bring the condemned man an extremely dry vodka martini on the rocks. He wiped his left eye with his tuxedo sleeve and brought into focus the Hollywood hills with their twinkling lights, a whore wearing sequins. How many hundreds of feet up am I, he wondered. His jacket and trousers were soiled and torn, and it annoyed him. He was a fastidious man. He was glad he wouldn't have to explain the condition of the suit to the haughty young man who had rented it to him.

"Have a nice day," the haughty young man had said to him as he pressed the elevator button.

No such luck.

He limped to the stone parapet and wondered about shouting for help. Not much hope and not much voice. Not much anything except what he knew was inevitable. He was going to be killed. He turned and faced the grillwork door. His ears strained for the sound of an approach on the stone staircase.

Maybe they lost me. Maybe they didn't see me stagger up here. Maybe they're too blind to follow the trail of blood I left. He coughed blood, and then wiped his chin, and then stared at the filth on his tuxedo sleeves. What a lousy way to treat madras.

He heard the hinges squeak on the grillwork door and looked up. His eyes wouldn't focus, but he knew someone had joined him. He could hear heavy breathing. He could sense the slow advance of his opponent.

"Don't kill him!"

It was a woman's voice he recognized. The voice was harsh and underlined with menace, but he recognized it. It was the voice of a soft and voluptuous woman who had greeted him earlier with warmth and friendliness.

"You damn fool! Don't kill him *here!"*

So much for warmth and friendliness, he thought, and then the brutal blow connected with his chin. It drove him back over the edge of the stone parapet, and he fought to maintain his balance.

"Oh!" he said with a faint sigh, "Oh, my."

He teetered on his back for a few seconds, and then felt a strong grip on his ankles.

"Don't do it, you fool! *Don't!"*

But he was already hurtling into space, never again to enjoy the first sip of an extremely dry vodka martini on the rocks.

The woman released her grip on the man's tweed jacket

and backed away slowly, trembling. He faced her and said with a controlled voice, "You'll catch cold up here."

"You'll catch worse for this," she said with a weak voice. "You will, you know. He won't like this. He won't like this at all. There was to be no violence here. He promised me that. It was part of our deal."

"It wasn't part of mine." He jerked his head toward the void that had been briefly filled by the doomed young man. "He could have finished us."

"You didn't have to kill him here!" Her voice had regained its strength, and he recognized the fire in her eyes. "The boys could have handled him. They know how to do these things."

"He saw me. He would have finished me."

"You didn't have to kill him here! We could have locked him up in the dungeon until the boys got back from Vegas. Oh, you are so tiresome!" She turned on her heel and clattered toward the grillwork door. There she turned and watched him struggling to light a cigarette in the fierce wind. "You don't even have the sense to do *that* indoors."

"You know there's only one thing I like to do indoors."

"You bungle that too." She turned and disappeared. He listened to the clatter of her heels on the stone stairs and then crumpled the cigarette in a beefy fist and sent it flying after the doomed young man.

The morning sun was fighting a losing battle against the smog blanketing Los Angeles. Detective Ira Sparks wiped his eyes with a handkerchief and then stared at the corpse sprawled like an idle puppet on the grass.

"Why do they dump everything in Griffith Park?" he said with a groan to his associate, Detective Boyd Gross.

"It's so convenient," replied Gross.

The coroner, Maurice Mosk, completed the swift preliminary examination of the corpse. "He's got an awful lot of broken bones. That's quite a beating he took. I'm sure he didn't die here."

"Maybe he was hit by a truck on the freeway," suggested Ira Sparks.

"What would a guy in a fancy madras tuxedo be doing on the freeway?" Boyd Gross wondered aloud. He examined the jacket label. "Gerber's. They rent these things. That should help trace him. There's nothing in his pockets but lint. No wallet, no letters, no nothing. He sure took a terrific beating. Look at that face. I'll bet it was handsome once."

Ira Sparks put his arm around the coroner's shoulder while the police photographer earned his salary. "Any ideas, Maurice?"

"I'll know better when I get him back to the morgue. But offhand, from the feel of some of those fractures, I'd say he might have fallen from quite a height."

"That happens to a lot of people in Hollywood."

The coroner looked into the detective's face. "I didn't know you were a philosopher."

Sparks crossed to Gross. "You take Gerber's. I'll get the stiff's prints and send them to Washington." He stared at the body. "Somebody sure had it in for him."

The 747 jet airliner was midway across Colorado when Norton Valentine decided he loathed the movie he was watching. The lady on his left was repairing her nails, and he wondered why the airlines hadn't thought of providing manicurists and barbers for first-class passengers. He removed his earphones and placed the apparatus at his feet.

"That piece of crap you've been watching has grossed over eight million to date."

Norton favored the lady with a smile.

"A monument to the bad taste of world film audiences," she continued, while emulating Picasso with her left thumb.

"Are you in films?" he inquired politely.

"Just because we're headed for L.A. doesn't mean I have to be in films." She examined the thumbnail and shrugged. "But in a way I am connected with the industry." She raised her window shade and then repositioned herself, facing Norton. "I'm Lila Frank."

Norton thought she expected a blare of trumpets. He smiled what his friends would call his practiced dumb smile. The lady leaned toward him as though to offer a challenge.

"Lila *Frank*."

"How do you do, Miss Frank," he said affably. "I'm Norton Valentine."

"Don't you *read* me?"

"Quite easily. I see a lovely brunette with beautiful skin, hazel eyes, full red lips . . ."

"You mean you never *heard* of me?" Everything about the lady was lovely except her voice. It was shrill and strident and should have been quoting a bargain in fish. "'Frankly Speaking'."

"Go right ahead. If anything I've said has offended you . . ."

"It's what you *haven't* said that's offended me, you boob." Then she wrinkled her nose and smiled. "You're pulling my leg."

"Later, if you're free."

"You *really* haven't heard of me." She spoke to the ceiling. "Syndicated in over two hundred papers across the world, a weekly television spot, and he hasn't heard of me. Well, so much for the power of the media." She examined his face. "Where you been living the past three years? Tibet?"

Norton leaned toward her cozily. "I don't read tabloids. I don't read gossip columns. I'm a stockbroker."

"Okay, Norton. I never knock money. Got any hot tips?"

He spread five fingers.

"Save them for your wife."

"I'm not married."

The film ended, and shades were raised, and the cabin brightened with sunlight. Lila pulled the zipper on her manicure case and tucked it into her alligator handbag. It gave her time to digest Norton Valentine. Probably in his mid-thirties with rugged good looks, traces of gray around his temples and even white teeth, and when he stood up, she was sure his frame would straighten into a lithe, lean, well-proportioned body. Some girl might strike it lucky tonight, if she liked the type. He wasn't Lila's type, but she was a trained inquisitor.

"In L.A. for a big deal?"

"Small deals are for telephones."

She lit a cigarette. "Anything to do with anybody important in Hollywood? You know, something I could use for my column?"

"The only thing I could offer for your column are punctuation marks."

She laughed despite herself. "How come it took until Colorado before we started talking?"

"I'm basically shy."

"Of what?"

Their stewardess interrupted with light refreshments. Lila waved her away with an impatient gesture that Norton was positive dried her fingernails.

"How'd you get into newspaper work?" Norton asked, looking genuinely interested.

"That story would take forever. I got the column by being in the right place at the right time." Norton wondered whose bed. "You know I'm pretty powerful out here."

"I hope it makes you happy."

"It makes me rich. At least we've got one thing in common. I invest my money carefully. Oh, stewardess! Are we arriving on time?"

"Looks good!" were the cheerful words that popped from the pretty, plastic face.

"Better get repaired," said Lila. Norton rose, and she glided past him with a friendly pat on his shoulder.

Norton settled back in his seat and stared out the window. Lovely brunette with lovely skin, hazel eyes, full red lips. Lovely woman.

Lovely Marti.

"I'm not married." Why did it still hurt when he said those words? I'm not married. I am two years and three months not married. I am no longer married to one of the most beautiful, voluptuous, sensuous women ever chiseled out of rock. Marti

Leigh, the enchanting tigress photographers fought to immortalize in celluloid. Marti Leigh, of whom one powerful advertising executive had said, "She could convince the great unwashed to brush their teeth with lye." Marti Leigh, whose eyes signaled Yes and whose lips could never say No. Marti Leigh, the cuddlesome bunny with morals to match.

Norton's film of memory screened an incident that had occurred four years before. He had met, pursued, wooed and won the glamorous Marti. The honeymoon in Nassau had been so idyllic, Norton considered selling the film rights. In Washington, D.C., Clay Stopley, Norton's closest friend and business associate gave the blissful newlyweds a dinner party. Marti was the center of attraction, and Norton stood to one side with Clay, admiring his glorious bride.

"She's too beautiful," commented Clay with admiration. "A wife like that would give me insomnia."

"Who sleeps?"

Clay looked at Norton with envy. "I suppose she's giving up her career to be housewife and mother. Another fallen sparrow."

"We haven't discussed it. She still has contracts to fulfill."

"If she was mine, I wouldn't let her out of my sight."

"I don't have your insecurities, kid. She can do anything that keeps her happy."

And Marti did everything that kept her happy, including a Republican senator, a halfback with the Green Bay Packers and Clay Stopley.

"Clay . . . my best friend . . . *Why?*"

Marti shrugged. "Because he was there."

The palm of Norton's hand connected with Marti's cheek. She staggered against the bedroom wall, tears stinging her eyes. She blinked rapidly and then folded her hands. "Why hit me? Hit him."

"I already have." He jerked a suitcase from the closet and tossed it on the bed. "You better see your lawyer. I've already seen mine."

"Did you hit him too?"

The jet hit turbulence, and Norton's stomach turned a somersault. The turbulence wasn't the reason; it was the memory of Marti.

"If you're going to be sick, would you turn away from my seat?" Lila was back and exquisitely repaired. With both her hands she held tight to the seat in front of him, as though trying to maintain her balance on a trampoline. Norton struggled to his feet as the FASTEN SEAT BELTS sign flashed on. Lila watched his frame straighten into a lithe, lean, well-proportioned body. I knew it, she thought to herself, just as I suspected. Surface perfection. His only incongruity was the absence of a boyish grin.

Settled in their seats with seatbelts fastened, Lila watched Norton light a cigarette. "How long will you be in L.A.?"

"For as long as I have to be."

"Where are you staying?"

"The Doheny Dauphin."

"Small, clean and unprepossessing. Hardly the flash for a stockbroker."

"I deal in small, clean, unprepossessing stocks. I don't suppose you're free for dinner tonight?"

"I'd like to be, but I'm not." She gave him her private phone number. "Call me tomorrow morning. I'll see when I can fit you in."

"You're too kind."

"Sorry. I didn't mean it to sound that way. I'm really a very busy lady. I mean, I just spent five days in New York on business, and there wasn't even time to get mugged."

Norton exhaled a perfect smoke ring. "Can you suggest some action in this town?"

"No friends? What about your business associates?"

"Tomorrow. It's been years since I've visited Hollywood. I'd like to look around. Oh I've been given some phone numbers, but like I said, I'm a little shy about using them."

"Nothing ventured, nothing gained. You weren't so shy about asking me out tonight."

"Well, we're old friends."

"Norton," said Lila blithely, "I think you're going to do just fine out here."

Norton removed his address book from his jacket breast pocket and began flipping pages. He studied some names and then asked Lila, "You probably know everybody. Who's Hagar Simon?" He glanced at her in time to see her face go rigid. "Your worst enemy?"

"What? Who? Hagar? Good Christ, no. Who gave you *her* name, of all people?"

"Friend of mine in New York. Harvey Tripp."

"Harvey Tripp," repeated Lila with mock awe. "You certainly know a lot of boys at the top."

"I get around."

"I can see you do. Didn't he tell you about Hagar?"

"Nothing much. Just that she's a great gal and throws some terrific parties. Her husband used to be a producer or something."

"Hardly 'or something.' Isaac Simon's a legend out here. Until the conglomerates squeezed him out and gave him his fatal heart attack, he was right up there on top with Sam Goldwyn and Louis B. Mayer. He created Hagar. Didn't you ever see any of her pictures?"

"Hagar *Simon?* Sorry. It doesn't ring a bell."

"Neither did she. She was Hagar Holt, the ice skater."

"Ohhhh, Hagar *Holt.* She used to be quite a dish."

"The hottest thing on ice. And still a very handsome woman." Lila examined her cuticle. "Couldn't make it as an actress, though. Poor Simon poured millions into her career, and that's what did him in with his stockbrokers. When he died five years ago, they were so broke, she was down to one cat."

"So who pays for her terrific parties?"

A wry smile appeared on Lila's face. "That's anybody's guess. Hagar's a smart lady. She managed to rise out of the ashes. I'm sure you know about her castle."

"You mean she really lives in a castle? I thought Harvey Tripp was kidding me."

"Oh, no. Hagar still owns the castle. Isaac Simon had it shipped piece by piece from France, when he still had that kind of money. The castle along with a lot of fancy tapestries and paintings, and God knows what else. Luckily for Hagar, it was all in her name and couldn't be touched when Isaac was forced into bankruptcy. After he died, she did some liquidating of her own, and then with the help of friends like Harvey Tripp, I suppose, she made some shrewd investments, and now she's truly the queen of her castle. The hostess with the mostess. Hagar commands, and Hollywood obeys. Party after party, a constant round, two or three a week at least. By all means get in touch with her. You don't have to be Jewish to be one of Hagar's chosen people."

"I suppose you've been to a lot of her parties."

Lila's eyes widened. "Of course, I have! I'm a reporter, and she's news."

"Harvey tells me those parties can get pretty wild."

"My lips are sealed." That'll be the day, thought Norton. Lila stared out the window. "Well, here we are. The neon graveyard." She turned to Norton. "My car will be waiting for me. Can I give you a lift to your hotel?"

"Thanks a lot, but I've ordered a rental car."

She studied him for a moment and then said, "I think you're a bit more important than you've let on. Harvey Tripp doesn't deal in nobodies."

"Are the important people the only ones who matter to you?"

"Not always, but I'm one of those girls who only shops the best labels."

"I can assure you my father didn't raise his leg against trees."

Lila patted his hand. "Call me tomorrow. We'll make a date. I like you."

Forty minutes later, Lila's chauffeur-driven Cadillac glided effortlessly toward her house in Bel Air. She sat on the plush backseat with one leg tucked under her, smoking a cigarette and stroking the chinchilla coat at her side. She stared out the window deep in thought, the subject under consideration being Norton Valentine. Handsome. Glib. Successful. Available. A likely catch for any girl out trawling.

Why haven't I heard of him before?

Lila snapped her fingers, reached for the telephone and dialed. After three rings, she heard a whiskey-soaked voice slur, "Hello?"

She purred, "Hello, Burton, darling."

The voice at the other end brightened. "Sweetheart! When'd you get back?"

"I'm in my car right now, heading for home. New York was ghastly, but mission accomplished."

"What's the word from the old man?"

"Tell you all about it when I see you. Now Burton put down your drink . . ."

"I'm not . . ."

"Put *down* your drink, and write down this name. Norton Valentine."

"What about him?"

"Do you *know* him?"

"Never heard of him. Who is he?"

Lila gently scratched a thigh. "That's what I want you to find out. I sat next to him on the plane. Quite a dish, but I wasn't hungry. He says he's a friend of Harvey Tripp's." She could hear ice cubes dropping into a glass.

"If he is, then he's somebody."

"But what kind of a somebody? He says Harvey told him to get in touch with Hagar."

"Harvey's most discreet about that."

"Exactly. I want you to check this guy out."

"Why? Did he rub you the wrong way?"

"Not yet. But I don't know. You know my instincts."

"I know your instincts," he repeated flatly. "Harvey's a hard guy to track down, but I'll get on it right away. What's this Valentine like?" Lila gave him the full description. "I'll try you later if I have anything. By the way, don't miss my column today."

"I read it on the plane. One of these days you're going to step over that dangerous boundary into libel."

"Balls. The Kennedy's are always fair game. Besides, my readers expect Burton Hartley to hit below the belt at least once a week. That's how I hold on to them. I shall now blow you a kiss and hang up."

Lila replaced the phone in the cradle and then stubbed out her cigarette. *That's how I hold on to them.* The statement she'd heard from beautiful downtown bourbon echoed in her mind. Poor old Burton, she thought with a weary sigh. Are you aware that your career hangs by a very slender thread? Do you know what persuasion it takes to keep your contract from being canceled? Probably. Why else soak your fantasies in alcohol? There are at least two friends left in your life who remain faithful. Me, Lila. And Hagar.

The Cadillac entered the driveway to Lila's estate, and two beautiful Airedales came bounding and yelping toward it. Lila lowered a window, stuck her head out, and shrieked with delight. "Seymour! Shirley! Your mommy's home. Oh, my beautiful babies, how I've missed you!"

From the bedroom of his ground floor suite in the Doheny Dauphin, Norton Valentine looked out at the bronzed bodies on display at the swimming pool. He was tempted to change into trunks, slide back the glass partition, and subtly position himself next to a silver blonde beauty who had caught his eye. But he remembered his priorities and crossed the room to the telephone. He sat on the bed and found the number he needed in his address book. He dialed, and after a brief interrogation by a male receptionist, he was connected with Detective Ira Sparks.

2

"If I was looking for a score, I'd go for that fat redhead in the psychedelic bikini." Ira Sparks stood at the window in Norton's living room, which also looked out on the swimming pool. Norton crossed to the detective's side, while buttoning his jacket, and stared at the obese subject under discussion.

"I'd make her take a saliva test," commented Norton. Sparks moved away from the window with a grin, while Norton followed him with his eyes. "What do those girls out there do besides exhibit themselves?"

"Oh, some of them are legit. Singers here for a recording date. New York actresses in for a tee-vee spot. Actors' wives. A few hookers. The usual afternoon crowd at a hotel swimming pool. The men start putting in an appearance around five. They're the ones whose hair is longer. Which reminds me," he said, glancing at his wristwatch, "we'd better get a move on if we want to catch Maurice at the ice palace." He answered Norton's questioning look. "The morgue. The deep freeze. Maurice Mosk is our coroner." He walked slowly to the door. "Your buddy's apartment was on the other side of the pool." He shook his head. "Funny how I couldn't recognize him when we found him in Griffith Park. Well, his mother wouldn't have known him, either, the way his face was bashed in. Still, I only met him once, and meeting someone once doesn't always register. Could have knocked me over when Boyd Gross got back from Gerber's with the stiff's . . . your friend's name." He shook his head again. "He should have kept in closer touch. I don't hold with the lone wolf act."

Norton said nothing and preceded Sparks out the door.

At the morgue, Maurice Mosk was wearing a white smock and eating an ice cream cone. Boyd Gross watched him with distaste as Ira Sparks entered with Norton.

"What kind of ghoul are you anyway?" Gross asked Mosk.

Mosk licked strawberry ice cream from his lips. "I didn't have any lunch. You expect me to go all afternoon without eating?"

"But in *here?*"

"You listen . . . when I was a medical student, I used to dissect a cadaver with my right hand and eat a corned beef on rye with my left."

"Did you ever get confused?"

Sparks interrupted and introduced Norton. Mosk crossed to the refrigerator locker and pulled out a shelf. Norton stared at the brown tag dangling from the big toe of the corpse's right foot. Clay wouldn't like that, he thought. Not brown, he loathed brown. Turquoise, maybe, or even orange, but brown he had found depressing. Norton's eyes traveled to the face, and he suppressed a shudder.

"Not very nice," said Mosk before popping the last of the ice cream cone into his mouth.

"Not nice at all," responded Norton huskily. "He was one hell of a great looking guy." He turned to Mosk. "Are you finished with him?"

"Unless you think he needs a pedicure."

"Not funny," snapped Sparks. To Norton, he said, "Where do we ship him?"

"His family's in Kansas. I'll give you all the particulars.

Better make sure he's in a sealed coffin. We'll trump up some reason. Car crash. Something like that. I wouldn't want his folks to see him like this. He was one hell of a good looking guy."

The four adjourned to Ira Sparks's office, where they huddled over containers of coffee. Mosk had memorized the deceased's bone breaks and fractures and recited them by rote. Norton listened in stony silence.

"And that's why I think he either fell or was pushed from some elevation," concluded Mosk.

"What about his face? Could the impact of a fall have done that much damage?"

"No. They rarely land face down. That was done with a blunt instrument, like maybe a rock. Lots of rocks in Griffith Park."

Norton turned to Sparks. "Find any rock out there with blood on it?"

"No, but we're still looking. Somebody with a good pitching arm could be giving us a hard time."

"I'm not finished," interjected Mosk. "There were other bruises on the neck, shoulders and torso that indicated he had taken a beating. His knuckles were scraped, which indicates he at least attempted to put up some defense. For good measure, I did an autopsy. He'd been doped, and a fair guess is it was a pretty heavy dose."

"Alcohol?" asked Norton.

"Oh, sure there was alcohol, but not enough for a conviction if he'd been pulled in for drunk driving."

"I wish he had been," said Norton before sipping some coffee.

"Gerber's wants to know who's going to pay for the tuxedo." Boyd Gross looked almost naively cherubic.

Norton sat back in his chair. "We'll take care of it."

We, thought Gross, who's this we? Who's this Norton Valentine? Who's the stiff? Who the hell was Clay Stopley?

Sparks interrupted Gross's train of thought as he addressed Norton. "I can have Stopley's suitcase brought up. I've gone over the contents myself. Nothing there of interest."

"No address book? Papers? Letters?"

"Nothing. It was clean. Like his body when we found him. No lead except the Gerber's label."

"That's pretty dumb of whoever did it." Sparks flushed slightly. "No offense, Ira. I mean whoever bumped him should have known he'd have been traced by either the label in his jacket or his fingerprints."

"Maybe they were just stalling for time."

"Maybe. Murderers do dumb things."

"I know," said Sparks softly.

Mosk was on his feet. "I've given you all I can contribute. I'll make the arrangements to have his body shipped home."

"You can go too, Boyd," directed Sparks. Boyd nodded and left with Mosk. Sparks settled back in his swivel chair, crossed one foot over the other and lit a cheroot. "I'd offer you one, but most people find cheroots repulsive."

"I'm one of them," said Norton, dropping his empty coffee container into a wastepaper basket. He rubbed his chin and then said, "You can release the news of Clay's murder to the newspapers. It's been two days since you found his body. Somebody must be suffering from a bad case of nerves wondering why Clay's death wasn't worth an item."

Will you see the item, Marti? Will you be shocked? Will you shed so much as a single tear? Or more likely will you say to yourself: "Stopley? Clay Stopley? Now that name sounds familiar."

"You said something?" Sparks was leaning forward with an anxious look.

"What?"

"Your lips were moving. I thought you said something."

"No, I didn't say anything. I was just thinking."

"I must say you guys have me puzzled."

Norton examined the tip of his sandal. "Sorry about that."

"I mean, I know you're mixed up somehow with the Feds. I have my orders to give you every cooperation. Yet your friend Stopley never asked for any cooperation."

"Maybe he didn't get the chance."

"I mean, just that one meeting with him at the hotel a couple of weeks ago, and that's all. I don't even know if he ever got inside Hagar's castle."

"I think he got inside," said Norton casually.

"You think, or you know?" Sparks dropped some ash on the floor with an exaggerated gesture.

"Clay was a very smart operator." He sank back in thought. He got inside, Mr. Sparks, and unless you're a big fool, and I don't think you are, you know he got inside. Just like I will get inside, either through my introduction from Harvey Tripp or through a young lady Clay was seeing here in Hollywood. Clay didn't like you, Mr. Sparks, and Clay liked just about everybody. That was his most serious shortcoming, but one overlooked that because he usually brought home the goods. *How* the hell was he tripped up, or *who* the hell did it?"

"Something you want to tell me?" asked Sparks abruptly. "I mean, whoever Clay Stopley was, it's still my murder case."

"I'm not forgetting that. But we have our orders too, you know." He favored the detective with his practiced dumb smile. "Sorry about that, but that's how it has to be."

Sparks responded with a Gallic shrug. "And I suppose now you storm the castle."

"Nothing so melodramatic. I'll be invited there. The way Clay was invited there."

Sparks crushed the cheroot in an ashtray with an angry movement. "If you know he's been there, why don't you come out with it and say so? Have you seen the place?"

"Not yet."

"It's an effing tall monstrosity, mister. It's a real honest-to-God castle. It's got turrets and stonework and ramparts, everything except the drawbridge and moat. You know how high ramparts are? Very high! A guy could get killed if he got dumped from one. Of course, it could have been an accident. Mosk tells us there was dope and alcohol in him. If he was at

Hagar Simon's Monday night, he just might have wandered up to one. It was a very foggy night on Monday, and there were strong winds. Maybe he got sick and leaned over one of those stone parapets, lost his balance, and toppled to his death."

"Maybe. And then Mrs. Simon, in fear of bad publicity, had his body removed, his personal effects cleared from his pockets, and then asked a good friend to dump him in the park and further complicate identification by bashing in his face with a rock. Get Burt Bacharach to write the score, and maybe we can take it on the road." Sparks looked apoplectic, and Norton put his stupid grin to work again. "Don't get mad. I'm more meticulous in my work than Clay Stopley. I'll be in frequent touch. In fact, I might even become a pest."

"That won't bother me."

"Did Mrs. Simon entertain Monday night?"

"She did. A small dinner party."

"Was Clay there?"

"She says he wasn't."

"Any idea as to the other guests?"

"Some. Burton Hartley, the columnist. Some Jap bigwig named Udo Yosaka."

"I know Yosaka. He operates mostly out of Hawaii. He's got a frozen-food plant there."

"That's Yosaka. The other names I got out of Mrs. Simon are Chloe Jupiter . . ."

"*Chloe* Jupiter? I used to cut school to see her pictures and then get beaten by my old man for having done it. Chloe was considered a very, very wicked lady."

"Chloe was with her niece, Viola Pickfair. She also calls herself an actress."

"If she's half as sexy as her aunt was . . ."

"She isn't."

"You know her?"

"I've seen her. I've seen them all. They also say Clay wasn't there that night."

"They could all be lying."

— 18 —

"They could be. Viola Pickfair admitted to having met Stopley once on a double date with a friend of hers named Karen Frost."

"Was Karen Frost at the castle Monday night?"

Sparks seemed chagrined. "It didn't occur to me to find out."

"It can wait. The Pickfair girl can probably tell me how to connect with her."

"You intend to interview all these people?"

"Not all. Just the Pickfair girl to start with. After all, I'm not a detective. I'm a stockbroker in town on business. I happen to have known Clay Stopley. We were at Rutgers together. I saw an item about his death in tomorrow's paper, right?"

"It'll be in."

"So I went to the police, met you, got what few facts you know, and decided to call on Miss Pickfair. With any luck, I might even take her to dinner."

"Luck will be on your side. She's a nut. She kept asking if I'd seen her three months ago on 'Charlie's Angels,' and when I told her I never saw the program in my life, she says, what do I mean I never saw the program why just about everybody in the whole United States and Canada watches that program and what kind of a creep am I who doesn't watch a program beloved by . . . Oh, my God, I've caught it from her." He was mopping his brow with a handkerchief. "Her aunt Chloe was another unusual experience, let me tell you. What with her gorilla . . ."

"A bodyguard?"

"A bodyguard, but a *real* gorilla." Norton's eyebrows went up. "His name's Irving."

"Gorillas can crush a man to death. Even a gorilla named Irving."

"I never even thought of that. I must be slipping. Chloe Jupiter is Hagar Simon's neighbor. I mean their estates are separated by some fifty acres or so but . . . Christ, this is too bizarre."

"Don't let it worry you. It's a little something to think about. There might be no connection whatsoever, unless Miss Jupiter travels with her gorilla."

"I'll look into it."

Norton was making notations in his little black book. "Viola Pickfair's address and phone number?" Sparks gave them to him. "Then there was Chloe Jupiter, Burton Hartley and Udo Yosaka. That's all?"

"That was all I got out of Mrs. Simon. I'm sure there were others there on Monday night, but I couldn't force the names out of her."

"Not even with gentle persuasion?"

"Wait until you meet Hagar Simon. You'll see for yourself."

"I'm champing at the bitch." He saw Sparks bite his lower lip. "Do profanity or puns offend you?"

"Hmmm? No . . . not at all. I was just remembering Hagar as I knew her many years ago. She was a warm, very friendly, very confused young lady. She'd just met her husband, and he'd thrown stardust in her eyes. He was a lot older than she, you see. At least thirty years. Hagar's mother pushed her into the marriage. The old lady's dead now. I worked some of her personal appearances. We used to do a lot of that stuff years ago. You know, official bodyguard brigade and all that. Backstage, Hagar was just one of the gang. Nice. Fun. Lots of laughs. I hate to think she's mixed up in anything illicit today."

"We don't know for sure, do we?"

"And you won't tell me what you guys suspect."

"Sorry."

"So am I." Sparks shifted his large frame and stared out the window, while Norton busied himself briefly with his notes. Occasionally Norton studied the preoccupied detective. He was well over six feet in height, surely by some four or five inches, and carried his big frame well. Probably in his middle forties, perhaps younger by a few years, with hands that resembled ham hocks. His clothes looked as though they had been unpacked that morning from a trunk that hadn't been opened in a decade, but then few police officers received sartorial awards. Norton wondered if there was a Mrs. Sparks and an assortment of offspring.

"Do us both a favor. Go easy." Sparks was lighting a fresh cheroot.

"On who?"

"I'm talking about you. I have a feeling you're smarter than your late friend was, but still . . . go easy. I'd hate to see you end up the same way."

"I plan not to, but then, the best laid plans . . . and all that jazz." Norton got to his feet. "I'll go for a drive now and do some thinking."

Sparks arose and held out his hand. Norton shook it. When Norton reached the door and opened it, Sparks said, "Was Clay Stopley really that close a friend of yours?"

"He sure was. I once caught him laying my wife."

Norton didn't wait for the detective's reaction and shut the door behind him. What he didn't see was the cheroot drop from Sparks's mouth onto the desk.

Half an hour later, Norton was steering the rented Renault along a secluded road in Coldwater Canyon. He had a reasonable idea as to the location of Hagar Simon's castle and wanted a look at it. It was on every tourist's itinerary and pinpointed on every map of the stars' homes sold throughout Los Angeles. While some maps were out of date and many stars had since moved on to other quarters or foreign locations, the houses remained, to satisfy the appetites of the insatiably curious. The car tooled along slowly, while Norton tried to erase from his mind the ugly sight of Clay Stopley's battered body. Pushed or fallen from a rampart? Crushed by a gorilla? Or theory X, the unknown, the surprise answer. His last contact with Clay had been six days before his death. It was the afternoon of the day of his first (perhaps his only?) invitation from Hagar Simon.

"I've been sweating it out for a week," said Clay over the telephone, "and I finally got the phone call this morning. It must have taken her this long to check my credentials." Clay had arrived in Hollywood as a friend of a "certain New Jersey magnate" who was having income tax troubles.

"Maybe it's the first party she's giving this week," suggested Norton.

"No, there was one three nights ago. It was written up in Lila Frank's column. By the way, Frank will be in New York in a couple of days."

"We know that. She's also booked for a quick trip to Europe."

"Whereabouts?"

"Don't know that, but we're working on it. These babies really give us a tough time, the way they camouflage their tracks. What about Karen Frost?"

"Delicious."

"I'm not asking how she tastes. I'm asking what you've gotten out of her."

"Everything I want except information. She met Hagar through hostessing at some of her charity things. Karen's a legitimate model and does occasional small parts as an actress."

"She's a very expensive call girl, and don't fall in love with her."

"I never fall in love. You know that."

Sure I do, old buddy.

"And another thing, Nortie, she hasn't charged me a nickel."

"Some guys are just plain lucky."

"By the way, tonight's dress up, and I didn't bring my tuxedo with me. Do I buy one or rent one?"

"If you buy, it's out of your own pocket; if you rent, it's out of ours."

"I'll rent. You know I loathe crap off the rack anyway."

"Are you in touch with Sparks?"

"Not since our first meeting. I don't think he's too bright anyway."

"He has a very good record."

— 22 —

"He intimates Hagar Simon is clean as a whistle."

"From where he sits, why not? He doesn't know what we know."

"And what do *we* know?"

"I hope we'll know more after tonight. Don't overplay it. Just ingratiate yourself with your hostess, and get what you can on the other guests. Don't go prowling around on your own. You taking Frost?"

"She's taking me. The invitation came through her."

"Interesting."

"She's gorgeous. What do I do if there's some sort of circus tonight?"

"Need I tell you?"

Clay emitted a lewd chuckle. "These are the kinds of jobs I *really* like."

"Clay, be very careful. This assignment's no lark. You're up against a very tough, very dangerous syndicate."

"You don't have to remind me," said Clay soberly. "I'm just humming to give myself courage. You intending to make contact with Lila Frank in New York?"

"Not unless it's accidentally. She's covered herself with three bookings out of New York back to L.A. next week. I'm booked on all three. Whichever she takes, I'll be on it, sitting right next to her."

"Careful. I'm told she bites."

"Keep in touch."

Keep in touch, but Clay never called again. That wasn't unusual. If there had been anything important, he would have heard. Or perhaps the idiot had decided to play the lone wolf until he discovered something spectacular. Well, he certainly discovered something. If he hadn't, he'd be alive today, enjoying the view with Norton. And the view was spectacular. Before him through a windshield loomed Hagar's castle, a formidable sight. He'd seen nothing like it since a boat trip up the Rhine shortly after his divorce from Marti. (Why the hell can't I rid myself of the memory of you, you stinking nymphomaniac!) Norton concentrated on the castle. It was all there as Sparks had briefly described it. The turrets, the ramparts, the parapets, plus an imposing ten-foot-high stone wall surrounding the vast acreage. And the castle was high. Very high. A good six stories in height. A man could get killed dropping from such a height.

Slowly, he drove past the main gates. They were sturdy iron grills and tightly shut. Just inside the driveway were opposing sentry boxes, and although there was no sign of life, Norton was positive they were occupied by armed guards. He accelerated his engine and sped onward.

Should he phone Lila Frank or wait until tomorrow morning as ordered by her? Tomorrow morning would do. Why, indeed, had he waited until they were over Colorado before attempting any conversation with her? She started it anyway. She had slept or feigned sleep for the first three hours of the flight. It gave him time to study her Latin good looks. She also didn't snore, which was a plus mark in her favor in Norton's book. Marti used to wheeze and snuffle a lot, and sometimes she even talked, which was Marti's second mistake. The first was doing what she talked about in her sleep. (Please go away, Marti. Where *did* you go? Why have you disappeared from the pages of *Harper's Bazaar* and *Vogue?* Are you remarried? Are you dead? Are you . . . *Oh, go to hell!*) Back to Lila Frank. Cute broad. Smart filly. What's her real name? Not Lila Frank. Lila Frank was created when her column was born, but who was she before then? Not a trace. Why the cover-up? Well, sweet Lila is undoubtedly giving equal time to the origins of Norton Valentine. That look on her face when he, not too gently, inquired about Hagar Simon. Hatred or caution? Hatred would help.

The guests at Hagar Simon's this past Monday night. Burton Hartley. Journalist. Commie hater. Kennedy hater. Roosevelt hater. Sot. Hack. His column is frequently gibberish, a pragmatic galimatias of hysterical gobbledygook meant to be a shrewd and sagacious analysis of world affairs.

The son of a bitch is probably still trying to decide between Al Smith and Herbert Hoover. Udo Yosaka. Japanese financial wizard. What do those factories of his process besides frozen foods? Hash? Heroin? Scopolamine? What? Viola Pickfair and Chloe Jupiter.

That's *got* to be Chloe's estate!

Norton was glancing out the right window at a lavish, pink, heart-shaped mansion. Heart-shaped! Leave it to Chloe Jupiter. Showmanship begins at home. He would have to meet Chloe. He could do that through her niece. She's Hagar's neighbor. She dines at the castle. She's a shrewd old owl. Nothing would escape her. Irving, the gorilla. Damn it. Could Chloe Jupiter be part of Hagar's action? He hoped not. She'd been his pinup girl at elementary school. He had her seductive portrait taped to the inside of the door of his gymnasium locker. Chloe Jupiter in *Belle Of The Brawl*. He'd seen that one six times.

There must have been others at Hagar Simon's that Monday night. There had to be. And Clay Stopley had to have been there too. It made sense. He could feel it. He steered the car toward Sunset Boulevard.

He hoped Karen Frost was listed in the telephone directory.

3

There was indeed a listing for Karen Frost in the telephone directory, but it turned out to be an answering service. "Sorry, but Miss Frost's private number and address are privileged information." Norton left his name, his phone number and the brief message that he was a friend of Clay Stopley's. Mr. Stopley had died tragically, and perhaps she hadn't heard. The telephone service operator clucked her sympathies and before disconnecting urged Norton to have a nice day. It seemed to Norton that everyone in southern California was desperate for everyone else to have a nice day, and if they heard they hadn't, Norton imagined, they erupted in prickly heat.

He stretched out on the living room sofa, hating to waste the evening. Patience was other people's virtue. There were so many leads to follow, so much to do. He had a private number for Hagar Simon, but it was too soon to use that. He knew it was politic to delay phoning Lila Frank until the next morning. He thought of trying to contact Burton Hartley, but after ten minutes of thought, he couldn't come up with a reasonable subterfuge for approaching him. He knew that very soon he would have to put his second cover story into operation. Norton Valentine as stockbroker would suffice for the moment, but eventually he would have to become the private investigator hired by Clay's family to investigate his horrible death. Clay's family had already been briefed, in case anyone tried to double-check.

Viola Pickfair? No. Scrub it. Let it wait until tomorrow. Don't push it. Go slow, he cautioned himself, go easy. Don't go out of your way to invite any sudden brushes with death like the one in Dallas after the Kennedy assassination.

He thought about Chloe Jupiter and smiled. He could still liberally quote dialogue from all of her films. He saw her on the witness stand in *The Men In My Wife*, irritated by a cross-examining defense attorney in the breach of promise suit reminding her of a former lover. "What wuz that name y'mentioned? Don Pedro San Alvarez? Hmmmmm . . ." Chloe examined the courtroom ceiling and then the all male jury as she seductively crossed a leg and stroked her long sable stole. She turned to the defense attorney, bristling with indignation, "Why shuah, I remember that there Don Pedro San Alvarez. Why he wuz'n' good enough tuh put in muh diary."

The telephone rang. Norton sat up. He let the phone ring two more times and then answered, "Hello?"

"Norton Valentine?" Very cool and sexy. He murmured acknowledgment. "This is Karen Frost. It's not true about Clay, is it?" She sounded genuinely concerned. Genuinely concerned or like an actress who deserved a better break than she'd been getting.

"Yes, it is, I'm sorry to say."

"But how awful." There was a slight choke in her voice, and Norton wanted to believe it was unrehearsed. "How did it happen? Was it a heart attack?"

"I'd rather tell you in person, if it's possible. I know Clay thought a great deal of you. He phoned me in New York about a week ago on some business."

"Did he? I don't think he ever mentioned you."

Norton put a smile in his voice. "He probably didn't want me flying out here to cut in on his time."

She sailed swiftly past the insinuation. "We only dated two or three times. He was such fun. So full of life."

"You wouldn't be free for a drink, would you?"

There was a long pause from her end, and Norton suspected she was having a conference. She finally replied. "I'm a bit tired. I just drove in from Palm Springs."

"Just one drink?" Norton persisted with charm. "I just got in myself a few hours ago. His family asked me to come out and . . . and see to the arrangements."

"Oh dear . . . look . . . give me an hour, okay?"

"Anything you say." He wrote down her address and then confirmed they would meet in an hour.

So she just drove back from Palm Springs and rushed straight to check her answering service. She's either a bad liar or suffers from an anxiety complex. Norton leaned back and planned his wardrobe for the evening. The interrogation he would extemporize.

"Burton do us both a favor. *Nurse* this one."

Lila Frank shoved the weak scotch and soda into Burton Hartley's outstretched hand and then stood back watching him down the first gulp. He looked like a desert rat who, after a week's wandering miraculously had stumbled across a water hole. The columnist's face was covered with a two-day's growth of beard, and his eyes looked like stained-glass windows. He looked old enough to have celebrated the first world war's armistice. He wasn't at all that old. Lila's face softened. She remembered this was the old pro who had trained her in the rudiments of gossip column writing. How to plant a blind item, how to hit a celebrity below the belt without hearing the cry of pain from their lawyers, how to wheedle secrets out of the Sphinx. She owed him, and Lila always paid her debts.

"Now, tell me what Harvey Tripp told you about Norton Valentine." She was getting into an overstuffed armchair that was badly in need of recovering. For five years she had pleaded with him to redecorate and refurnish his home, but it was easier to get Hartley to part with a confidence than with cash.

"I didn't talk to Harvey Tripp. I talked to Phyllis Grain, his secretary."

"Where's Tripp?" she asked sharply.

"Off in parts unknown. What difference does it make? Miss Grain is attached at his hip. She's been with him since Moses parted the Red Sea. She okayed Valentine."

"How okay?" She glanced impatiently at her wristwatch.

He leaned forward slightly and inquired woozily, "Did you say you had a date?"

"Yes, I said I had a date, Burton. I'm meeting Czardi at the Greek Theater in half an hour."

"Oh? What's on there?"

"Four Fokine ballets. Now, come on, let's get back to Valentine." She hated herself for being impatient with him, but she knew his continued lucidity was now a matter of minutes.

"Oh, yes, Norton Valentine." He stared into his drink, as though Norton's credentials were being teleflashed there. "He's with Brixton and Sons, and you know where they stand on Wall Street."

"Go on."

"He goes by the title of Securities Analyst, which means he does a lot of dirty work. Hatchet man. He can manipulate a stock to look good, or he can send it plummeting. If he's for you, you get rich; if he's against you, you get headlines. The S.E.C. can't get a thing on him."

"He sounds like a presidential candidate."

"Miss Grain has no information, of course, as to his mission in Los Angeles, except be nice to him and try and find out what he's up to, because whatever it is could certainly be of use. Shall I pass this on to Hagar?"

"You'll pass out before you can pass on."

"Don't be cruel. Please don't be cruel."

"I'll phone Hagar in the morning. Now why don't you be a good boy and eat something and go to bed."

His eyes misted with tears as he slumped down in his chair, but his grip on the glass remained firm. "Can't eat . . . can't sleep. I'm so frightened . . ."

"Of *what*, for crying out loud! I told you you're safe. Your contract's renewed for another year, though God knows it took a lot of persuasion."

"Thank you, sweetheart. I can't thank you enough. I know it wasn't easy for you. My stuff's so old hat. So dull. So trite. I don't even get hate mail anymore. And all this . . ."

"All what?"

He placed the glass on a table. "Oh, for Christ's sake, don't horse around with me. You know what I'm talking about. Clay Stopley!"

"Very tragic."

His drunken voice overlapped hers. "I could tell that cop knew I was lying. I could see in his eyes he knew Stopley was at Hagar's Monday night."

"Did he press you?"

Hartley's voice grew indignant. "Of course he didn't press me! He wouldn't dare. I'm Burton Hartley, I'm . . ." He ran a hand over his face and then leaned back with exhaustion. "Why do I give a damn about the column? I've got all the money I need. Why don't I just retire gracefully and dictate my memoirs? When I was watching Winchell's decline, I swore then I'd never let myself in for that kind of humiliating experience. I told myself I'd quit while I was still on top." He emitted a dry chuckle. "Too late for that, isn't it? Would you find me ungrateful if I tendered my resignation to the proper authority?"

"I wouldn't find you ungrateful, I'd say you were a damned fool. Your column serves a very important purpose."

He raised his hand in a theatrical gesture. "My column is but a garden of evil in which certain items of a dubious and harmful nature are very carefully planted and nurtured. Sweetheart, there are any number of other inkstained prostitutes of the Fourth Estate who would leap at the chance to replace me and obey instructions faithfully."

Lila leapt to her feet with her eyes aimed at his face and her mouth open to fire. "I broke my back to get the old man to hold on to you, and you're staying!"

"Don't shout. You're making my ice cubes melt."

"There's no replacing you now, and you damned well know it. There's nobody else we know of we can trust, and there's no time to look for him. That was the argument I used, and by God, you're going to back me up or . . ."

". . . Or?"

Her anger abated, and a twinkle came to her eyes. She placed her hands on his shoulders and lightly kissed his cheek. "Or I'll hire you a trained nurse, and make you go cold turkey."

"Fat chance," he said with a snort. She moved away from him and gathered up her evening bag and gloves. "Who'd you say you were meeting?"

She sighed and told him, "Mickey Czardi."

"Ah yes. Count Miklos Czardi. I do hope his company is more palatable than the dreadful cuisine he serves in his restaurant."

"He only sells it. He doesn't eat it."

"I remember him when he was a man without friends or credit cards."

"Hungarians don't need friends, and they print their own credit cards."

"Won't his glamorous girl friend be with him tonight?"

"No, darling. You know how it is in this town. Two's company; three's a coproduction." She headed for the door.

"I love you, Lila."

She opened the door and said over her shoulder, "Likewise, darling. Talk to you in the morning."

Hartley didn't hear the door shut. He sat staring with glazed eyes at the palm of his limp right hand, as though hoping to read among the lines some sign of a brighter future.

Norton Valentine locked the Renault, pocketed the keys, crossed the street, and walked up the short drive that led to the entrance of the apartment building on North Kings Road. It was a new building, and a large sign out front advertised eagerly for prospective tenants. It offered such enticements as bedroom and den, two fireplaces in every apartment, air conditioning, a sun patio with swimming pool, free gas and twenty-four-hour doorman. Probably everything about the sign was true except the last item. There was no doorman. Norton found Karen Frost's name on the roster in the foyer and pressed her bell. In response to her inquiry on the intercom, he identified himself. He heard the clickety-click releasing the lock on the door to the lobby, and he entered.

"This way!" he heard her shout and turned left past an elevator down a hallway that had probably been designed and decorated by Salvadore Dali. Ahead of him, he saw standing in a doorway a tall, slender redhead wearing oatmeal lounging pajamas and a pair of oversized dark glasses. Norton knew he wasn't sick, but she was just what the doctor ordered.

Karen Frost watched him approach with a wan smile on her face. What she saw was better than she had expected, though sandals, tight blue jeans and safari jacket didn't quite go with her image of an important young stockbroker. "Hello, Mr. Valentine," she said, in a voice coated with caramel, and held out her hand.

Norton clasped her hand and said, "Thanks for letting me come over."

"Not at all," she replied, moving slightly to make room for him to enter. He brushed past and caught a whiff of expensive, exotic perfume. She shut the door and then preceded him into the living room. "I've just moved in a few weeks ago, so please forgive the mess. What are you drinking?" She crossed to a bar in the corner of the room, the shelves of which looked as though they had been stocked by an alcoholic expecting a shortage.

"Would a margarita be too much trouble?"

"Now isn't that funny? I was just thinking of having one myself." She reached for a bottle of tequila and a pitcher and began mixing the drinks. "Be a doll, and do the salt on the glasses."

"Where's the salt?"

"Right here." She reached under the counter and produced an apothecary jar filled with salt. Norton spread salt on a dish and deftly coated the rims of the glasses with a professional twist of the wrist, while wondering if her dark glasses were an affectation or a curtain behind which were hidden unmentionable secrets. The expression on her face as she lazily stirred the contents of a pitcher belonged on Mount Rushmore. Karen broke the conversational deadlock. "Tell me about Clay." He told her what he knew without sparing the more gruesome details. As he spoke, her hand began to shake, and then she released her hold on the stirrer and clamped her hand over her mouth, turning away from him.

"I'm sorry. I should have edited some of the details." He watched her lift the glass and dab at her eyes with a cocktail napkin. "When did you last see him?" He was working hard at keeping his tone casual.

"Last Thursday night, I guess it was. I left for Palm Springs the next morning. I posed for a fashion layout there." Composure regained, she poured the drinks and led the way to a sofa.

"Did he happen to mention an invitation to Hagar Simon's for Monday night?"

She hesitated for a moment and then said, "Not that I remember." Norton knew she wished she sounded convincing. "As far as I know, he's only been to Hagar's once, and that was as my escort."

"How'd you meet Clay?"

"A mutual friend of ours in New York told him to look me up. He caught me on a very lonely night, and so I accepted his invitation to dinner."

"I can't imagine you having many lonely nights."

"You'd be surprised." She faced him with a winsome

expression. "There's a surplus of single women in this town."

"I should think you'd be in a position to pick and choose your dates."

"Mr. Valentine," she said wearily, drawing out his name with mock exaggeration. "I am a mere mortal. A spinster by definition, not by choice. And I know you know more about me than you've let on. You told me Clay telephoned you, and it isn't ego that makes me assume I was probably Topic B, C or D in his conversation. I'm a party girl, and sometimes there's a fee attached to the festivities. When it's someone as attractive and as affable as Clay Stopley was, then it's sometimes on the house. I liked the guy. I liked him very much. Given the time and the opportunity, I might have grown to like him too much. Scrub that questionable look from your face, Mr. Valentine. I also have my dreams. My cottage doesn't have to be vine-covered, but I insist on at least two bathrooms and a man who remembers to drop the seat. How's the drink?"

Norton sipped without moving his eyes from her face. "Very good."

"Clay would say it was perfect. To me a word like 'perfect' makes all the difference in men. Are you a very successful stockbroker, Mr. Valentine?"

"How'd you know I was a broker? She hesitated for a moment and then favored him with a bland smile. "You said Clay phoned you on business. Stocks were his business, so my assumption should be valid."

"Score one for you. Now how's about scoring one for me? Have dinner with me."

"I'm sorry. I have a previous engagement. But there's no hurry. I said I'd phone when you leave." She rubbed some salt on a fingertip and sensuously licked it.

He drawled slowly, "The police think Clay was murdered." Her body went rigid. "Beaten up and pushed from a height. I drove past Hagar's castle earlier today. A fall from one of those ramparts could be fatal. I think he was at Hagar Simon's Monday night."

"Is that what the police think?"

"They interrogated Mrs. Simon and four of her guests. All of them insist Clay wasn't there."

Her body relaxed. "Well then . . ."

"I think it's a conspiracy of silence. There were probably other guests besides these four. I suppose Ira Sparks—he's the detective handling the case—didn't press for the rest of the guest list because he figured he'd get the same discouraging results."

"Oh dear, why do so many people find the truth discouraging?"

"Why would so many people agree to a lie?"

"Mr. Valentine . . ."

"Please call me Norton, Miss Frost."

"All right, Norton," she said melodiously, "why would so many people conspire to a lie?"

"Because murder can have such disagreeable consequences. 'Scandal' is an unpleasant word in everybody's vocabulary. Hagar Simon's guest lists are a homogeneous variety of the famous and the infamous."

She drained her glass and then said, "You know so much about Hagar. Is private investigating one of your hobbies?"

"No, but I get around. I meet a lot of people. I've met people who've been to Mrs. Simon's parties. I've had an earful. Do you like the woman?"

"There are things about her I admire."

"Such as what? Her wealth? Her position? Her parties?"

"Mostly her needlepoint," she replied sarcastically.

Norton smiled. "You're a real cool chick." With a lightning movement, he removed her dark glasses.

"*Hey!*" she yelped and jumped to her feet, the glass slipping from her hand and shattering on the floor. There was an ugly bruise around her right eye.

"Don't step on any glass," he cautioned her.

"That wasn't very nice, *Norton*."

"Neither's your eye. That birdie looks about two or three days old."

"Should I bake it a birthday cake?" she shouted. He wondered if she was being measured on the Richter scale, as she booted the glass fragments under the sofa. "Oh the hell with it!" She crossed back to the bar for a fresh glass and filled it.

"You're forgetting the salt."

"Ah, that's just a crappy affectation."

"Who hit you?"

"I fell off a horse in Palm Springs."

"You should have had it shot."

"I'm never cruel to dumb animals," she said while stirring her drink with an index finger, "even when they've been cruel to me."

"A short while ago, I was admiring the honesty of your thumbnail autobiography. Why don't you level with me about the mouse?"

She braced her back against the bar with one ankle crossed over the other. "Who are you, Norton? What's this all about? Are you Clay Stopley's grieving buddy and associate, or are you some new breed of private eye? If Clay was murdered—as you claim the police believe—on Monday night, why hasn't it made the newspapers?"

"Tomorrow. Clay's body was clean when they found him. No identification. I'm in Los Angeles because I was scheduled to join Clay today for a business conference. I'm snooping because I think the cops are acting a little lackadaisical. Frankly, I was wondering if your black eye was a farewell gesture from Clay."

"Clay's gestures were never painful," she said with an unbecoming leer. Then, as though quickly aware of her unwitting vulgarity, she apologized. "Sorry. I didn't mean that. It was a fit epitaph for him. I can't tell you anything else."

"Can't or won't?"

"Please go."

"I'll meet your price." He ducked as her glass came hurtling past his left ear. He heard it shatter against the wall behind him and then got to his feet, hands raised with open palms in defeat. "Okay, okay! I'm going! Reluctantly, but I'm going." She had hurried to the door and now pulled it open with a violent jerk. Norton strolled casually to the exit.

"Sorry about that smartass crack."

"Get out of here!" Her left hand connected with his back with surprising strength, and he stumbled into the hall, the door slamming shut behind him.

"Norton," he said to the ceiling, "that was very poorly handled."

"I don't see any Norton," said a concertina voice behind him. He turned and looked into the face of a snub-nosed, raven-haired pixie wearing slacks and a see-through blouse.

"*I* am Norton," he said, with his arms folded.

"You shouldn't go around talking to yourself because people who talk to themselves are the cruel victims of a loneliness syndrome and that could lead to serious injury to the psyche and the id and a one-way ticket to cuckoo land . . ."

"Oh, God, spare me," he gasped and rushed past her. Had he been in less of a hurry, he would have seen her press the bell to Karen Frost's apartment and then babble to a furious Karen when she opened the door, "So who was the john named Norton who talks to himself outside your door wearing those obscene blue jeans with thighs that look hard enough to crack coconuts and Jesus you're breaking my wrist . . ."

Karen pulled her inside and slammed the door hard.

Norton pulled away from the curb and headed toward Sunset Boulevard. There were no people strolling on North Kings Road, and the only sign of activity was the white Thunderbird behind him, which he saw in a glance at his rearview mirror. He shifted his thoughts to Karen Frost. That early surface innocence had brilliantly masked a poisonous flower. That hard shove out the door. That's big strength for a little lady. The sudden eruption of violent temper caused by an ungracious remark. But what kind of counterviolence could a sock in the eye awaken in her? A violent shove that could have sent Clay Stopley to his death? He couldn't recall Clay ever having punched a lady, but then Clay didn't tell him everything. He certainly hadn't told him about Marti, but then who tells a best friend he's banging his wife? Some guys wait until they know a divorce is imminent, some guys like Clay. And some guys like Norton can forgive that sort of betrayal in a friend, especially when you realize the friend has more to offer than the wife. Take this mental note, Norton, check up on Karen Frost's weekend in Palm Springs. In the morning call Ira Sparks . . . he paused to think . . . no, not Ira Sparks. Have one of our own boys do it.

He cruised along Sunset Boulevard looking for a place to eat. The white Thunderbird was still reflected in his rearview mirror. Other cars were going past in the adjoining lanes, but the Thunderbird was holding a steady pace behind Norton's Renault. How very interesting, thought Norton. There were two men in the Thunderbird. Very interesting indeed. Am I being tailed? If so, by whom, and on whose orders? Could they be plainclothes cops assigned by Ira Sparks for my protection? How very thoughtful, if they are, and if they are, how dumb of Ira not to have told me.

Norton decided to test the Thunderbird. He turned left into Doheny, heading back to his hotel. The Thunderbird followed. Norton drove into the garage under the hotel, pulled up and waited. The Thunderbird didn't follow him in. He turned off the ignition, left the car unlocked and took the elevator to the lobby. There he paused at the newsstand, selected a girlie magazine from a rack, and flipped pages, while surreptitiously casting an eye toward the window fronting the street. There was no sign of the Thunderbird. He replaced the magazine and crossed to the desk for his key.

In his kitchenette, he mixed himself a vodka and tonic and then made a phone call requesting the check on Karen Frost's purported assignment in Palm Springs. Then he sat staring out the window at the swimming pool. He wished there was somebody out there he could talk to. He hadn't felt this lonely since the day his divorce decree became final.

Count Miklos Czardi was looking across the table with displeasure at Lila Frank. They were seated in a circular booth of his restaurant facing the crowded bar. His frown intensified as she continued to ignore him, her eyes scanning the room for celebrities, while his anger gave a saturnine cast to his fading Magyar looks.

"Isn't it enough you dragged me out of the theatre in the middle of the Black Swan pas de deux without compounding the felony by ignoring me in my *own* restaurant?"

"I've seen better dancing by paraplegics," she said offhandedly, while drumming the table top with her fingers.

"Would you like another drink?" he asked with irritation.

"I haven't started this one."

"Shall we order dinner?"

"After I finish the drink."

"You're behaving objectionably."

She stared at him with hooded eyes. "Stop pushing me."

"I don't like being ignored. What's the matter with you tonight?"

She placed an elbow on the table and cupped her chin with the hand. "Heavy heavy hangs over my head. Ever experience the feeling?"

"Many times," he countered with an imperious sniff. "When my father lost his vast estates in Transylvania, and we had to flee the Nazis in an oxcart . . ."

"Oh, save that crap for Radie Harris."

"You never believe anything I tell you." He allowed himself a dramatic pause and then spoke with a tear in his voice. "Poor Daddy . . . killed by a bayonet thrust through the straw at the border . . ."

"Your father died of an abcessed fang."

"You're close," he said warmly. "Actually, it was a gangrene infection from an injury suffered from a disgusting habit of clipping his toenails with a rusty paring knife."

"In some Brooklyn tenement."

"Bronx."

Lila occupied herself with systematically crumbling a breadstick. "What happened at Hagar's Monday night?"

"Nothing while I was there. I left early. Anyway, why ask me? You could go straight to the horse's mouth."

"The horses were out of the stable when I called. I left messages. That was a bad mistake, killing Stopley."

"Indeed it was," he agreed airily. "He was so handsome and charming, a social asset." He nodded to a group of four middle-aged men at an adjoining table. They were a dour-looking lot in clothes of varying dark shades. Czardi said to Lila, "Some friends of yours. You might manage a smile for them." Lila looked at the four men and embraced them all with a wink.

"Why don't they learn to sit in the back?"

"Czardi's does not discriminate." He signaled the waiter to clear up the mess Lila had made with the breadstick. "Anyway, they sit where they like. They own enough of the place."

"Will there be anything else?" asked the waiter. Czardi shook his head, and the waiter left.

"I'm worried about Burton. I went to bat for him, and he's cracking up. When will I stop letting my heart rule my head?"

"You can't still be in love with him."

"Of course not. But you know the one about the weakest link . . ."

"Perhaps he needs a vacation. Perhaps . . . Hawaii?"

Lila regarded him sternly. "Don't you ever suggest that! Not ever for Burton!"

"Temper, temper!"

"Don't you temper me, your bogus highness! One of these days, they'll catch up with you and your phony immigration papers . . ."

"For God's sake, lower your voice." He made a lavish

gesture of straightening his bow tie. "I'm a highly honored and respected citizen of my adopted country . . ."

"Oh, shut up, and get me another drink. This one tastes like piss." A waiter responded to Czardi's signal in a flash.

"I think we should also order some food," insisted Czardi. Lila snapped at the waiter, "Bring me a club sandwich, and leave out the club." Czardi ordered a minute steak, and the waiter left. Lila lit a cigarette and resumed her celebrity spotting, while Czardi beamed at the crush at the bar.

"Business is magnificent tonight. I wish I could keep every nickel of it."

"You keep enough," drawled Lila, "Heifetz would envy the way you fiddle your books."

Czardi ignored the insult and espied a celebrated film star standing near the cashier's desk. "That woman with Roy Hunter looks like his father."

"Where's Roy Hunter?"

"They're near the cashier's desk."

Lila leaned forward and squinted. "That *is* his father." And then her range of vision encompassed a familiar figure perched on a stool at the far corner of the bar. "Well, well, well," she muttered.

"Well, well, well, *what?*"

"Norton Valentine's at the bar."

Czardi levitated and craned his neck. "Which one? The white turtleneck in the far corner?" Lila nodded. "I wonder why the dumb grin on his face."

"Looks like he's trying to make it with the brunette gargoyle wearing the hot pants."

"Oh, yes. She's one of our regulars."

"She looks so dear," said Lila with a tinge of venom.

"She's very dear," Czardi confirmed, "but she'll come down in price."

Norton wasn't in the least bit interested in the brunette. He was studying two men at the opposite end of the bar who had followed him into the restaurant. Their white Thunderbird was several spaces away from his car in the parking lot behind the eatery. They had mysteriously reappeared like science fiction mutations while he was tooling along Santa Monica Boulevard, looking for the celebrated Czardi's. Norton was beginning to enjoy the game. The men were drinking beer, which told him a lot. Both were in their late twenties or early thirties, and the taller of the two, the one with red curly hair wearing a maroon jacket and beige slacks, gave Norton the impression of an aborted prizefighting career in his past. His nose must have been broken at least twice, and his ears would have been more appetizing with dollops of melted cheese. His companion was under six feet in height and wore a tan jumpsuit with a green carnation pinned to his left lapel. He was leaning against the bar with a glum, bored expression, occasionally stealing a glance at Norton. From time to time, he ran his hand over his thinning blond hair, which hung like a bamboo curtain down to his ears. Norton decided the blond would be happier in a garage overhauling a faulty automobile engine. Norton's train of thought was derailed by a diminutive waiter who handed him a folded slip of paper. Norton read the brief note and smiled to himself. In answer to Norton's query, the waiter pointed to Lila and Czardi. He picked up his vodka and tonic and threaded his way to the circular booth.

Lila favored Norton with a dazzling smile as they shook hands and she introduced him to Czardi.

"*The* Miklos Czardi?" asked Norton as he settled next to Lila.

"There *are* no other Miklos Czardi's!" exclaimed the restauranteur with regal elegance and then signaled for a fresh round of drinks.

"There certainly aren't," added Lila, "because sometimes God is good." Of Norton she asked, "Been up to anything interesting?"

Norton decided to throw caution to the winds. "Well, actually, I had a rather sad experience."

"You saw *Moment By Moment?*"

"No, Miss Frank. One of my business associates was murdered Monday night." He saw Czardi go pale, while Lila mustered an expression of shock on her face that could have done with additional rehearsal. "I had to go to the morgue to confirm the identification. It was a brutal sight. His name was Clay Stopley."

"Clay Stopley . . . Clay Stopley . . ." Lila repeated the name, as though she hoped to build up an immunity to it. "Mickey? Didn't we meet a Clay Stopley at Hagar's a couple of weeks ago?"

Czardi intertwined his fingers and clenched them tightly. "Yes, as a matter of fact, I think we might have."

"He was with a girl named Karen Frost," said Norton helpfully.

"Of course!" Lila shook her head sadly. "Now I remember him. Such a good-looking guy, too."

"He's lost those looks," said Norton and, with subtle sadistic relish, described the corpse as he had seen it at the morgue.

"Oh, my God," gasped Lila, while clutching at her throat, "cancel my sandwich. How terrible for you, Norton. How really terrible. Now, I remember. He was in Wall Street too. I remember overhearing him advising someone to dump their Columbia Pictures stock. Dave Begelman, as I recall." She placed a damp palm over Norton's hand. "You poor guy. I hope this doesn't upset the deal you're working on."

Norton patted her hand gently while the waiter served the fresh drinks. "No, but it does complicate matters a bit. Most of the information I needed was in poor Clay's battered head."

Lila withdrew her hand and gazed at Czardi. "Mickey, darling, you're perspiring. Why don't you have them turn up the air conditioning?"

Czardi dabbed at his forehead with a napkin. "I wonder if Karen knows."

"She does," said Norton. "I had a drink with her at her place."

"Oh did you?" Lila toyed with her pearls. "Was she very upset when you told her?"

"Yes. She dropped a glass."

I hope that's all she dropped, thought Lila.

"By the way," continued Norton, "you wouldn't happen to know those two guys at the far side of the bar, would you?" He pointed out the maroon jacket and the jumpsuit. Lila shrugged innocence.

Czardi made a vague gesture. "I think they've been in before. Nobody important. Why?"

Norton smiled his dumb smile. "They've been tailing me for the past couple of hours."

"*Tailing* you?" squeaked Lila. "Why should anybody be tailing *you?* Unless they're from Bache and Company."

"I spotted them after I left Karen Frost's. They work in a white Thunderbird."

Czardi commented with a look of distaste, "Thunderbirds are for television producers."

"Now, Norton," began Lila, sounding like a patient school teacher, "we understand you've undergone a traumatic experience today, but surely there's no need to get neurotic about it."

"I could be wrong," said Norton genially. "It's probably just a coincidence that they followed me to my hotel and then picked me up again while I was looking for this place."

"Absolutely," agreed Lila. "Hollywood is a hotbed of coincidences. By the way, who downtown's investigating your friend's death?"

"A detective named Ira Sparks. He calls it murder."

"Murder," echoed Czardi eerily, going pale again.

"Yes, it certainly is murder in this place tonight," babbled Lila. "Just look at you, Mickey. You're positively melting. Are you too chintzy about that air conditioning? Waiter! *Waiter!* Yes, *you.* Go tell the maitre d' to turn up the air conditioning. Poor Mickey, you look as though you just left Shangri-La. Murder, Norton? Why would anybody want to murder Clay Stopley? I got it!" She snapped her fingers. "Jealousy. Karen has a string of johns who would kill for her. By God, I'm famished, where the hell's that club sandwich? *Ahhhh!* Can't you feel those fresh currents of cool air?"

"Funny, Lila, I'm only getting a lot of hot air."

"Norton, I think there's more to you than meets the eye." She leaned toward him cozily. "Come on, be good to a news hen. What's the *real* story? I haven't had a decent scoop since I bought some ice cream a couple of weeks ago. I know Ira Sparks. He's a-okay in my books. If you don't level with me, he will."

"So help me, all I know is what I've told you," insisted Norton, hoping it sounded sincere. "The only thing I've left out is the possibility he might have been at Hagar Simon's the night he was killed." He wasn't sure if Czardi had squelched a belch or was still fighting for air. Lila's eyebrows were rising slowly, and Norton wondered if they would join her hairline.

"What does Hagar say?"

"She says no." Norton told her about Hagar and the four guests.

"Well, if they say he wasn't there, then, darling Norton, he certainly wasn't there." One of her hands was out of sight under the table, and Norton wondered if her fingers were crossed. "How'd you know about Karen Frost?" Norton repeated an abridged version of his phone conversation with Clay Stopley the previous week. Lila's hand surfaced and patted Norton's cheek. "You leave the investigating to the professionals. Ira doesn't look like much, but he delivers. And as to those two bums trailing you, just tell Ira. If they are, he'll get them off your back."

"Oh, I don't mind them," said Norton with his stupid grin. "I think they're kind of fun. I wonder if either of them plays Scrabble."

Lila grinned. "Norton, you're real cute. I'm glad we ran into each other tonight." She turned to Czardi. "Wasn't I lucky sitting next to him on the jet?" She smiled at Norton. "Now you don't have to phone me tomorrow morning. We can make a date for dinner right now."

"Well, if we do, it'll have to be a tentative one."

"Why?"

"Well, I promised old Harvey Tripp—you remember my mentioning Harvey on the plane—I promised old Harvey I'd ring Hagar Simon. Frankly, I'm more curious than ever to meet her now."

Lila's eyes resembled a cobra's. "Of course, you are. As a matter of fact, she's throwing a little wingding tomorrow night. I'm invited. Would you like to escort me?"

"I'd be delighted." Very delighted, so delighted that I hope Hagar Simon knows she's throwing a wingding tomorrow night. And poor Miklos Czardi is having a coughing fit. Norton handed him a glass of water. "This should help."

"Your friends at the bar are leaving," said Lila. Norton turned and watched them depart. "You see? It was all in your mind. And goodness, Mickey! Look who's arrived! That's Mickey's girlfriend chatting with the matire d'. Isn't she gorgeous? Mickey met her in Hong Kong last month and absolutely hypnotized her into coming back stateside with him. Well, Norton, I can see you agree with me. Will you just look at Norton? He's positively mesmerized! She sees me! Yoo-hoo! You look absolutely *gorgeous*, darling! Norton, I'd like you to meet Marti Leigh."

4

Slowly, Norton got to his feet, terrified that at any moment they might buckle. His temples throbbed, and his mouth felt paralyzed. He'd often wondered how he would react should this moment arrive, and now the moment was here, and his behavior was nothing like the mental image he had prepared for himself. He was neither suave nor blasé and couldn't think of a quip with which to put them both at ease. He held his hand out stiffly, and she brushed it lightly with her fingertips, a polite smile on her face, her eyes gently mocking.

"How nice to meet you," purred the enchanting tigress as she squeezed in next to Czardi. "I didn't hear your last name."

"Valentine," he said swiftly and sat down. *I didn't hear your last name.* I thank you for that, sweetheart. I thank you for not giving the game away. I thank you for waiting until I get a chance to explain, if I get the chance to explain.

And then he thought of something that made his blood run cold. She knows these two extremely well. She would know Hagar Simon. She might have been at the castle Monday night. If she was, she might have seen Clay. And if she had . . .

"Palm Springs was hell," he heard her telling the others.

Czardi looked perplexed. "Palm . . ."

". . . Springs," interjected Marti swiftly. "Didn't you miss me?" Czardi grunted, and Norton suspected Marti's leg had connected with his shin under the table. Marti sought Norton's attention. "I was there on a modeling job with a friend of mine, Karen Frost. My first job in years. I'll never do it again, so help me." She took a sip of Czardi's drink. "Nice. Order me one, will you darling?" Czardi signaled a waiter, barked the order, and then settled into silence while Marti continued talking, this time aiming her mouth at Lila. "Karen phoned me a little while ago. She told me some awful news about her friend, Clay Stopley."

"We've heard it," said Lila almost inaudibly.

"Bad news certainly travels fast," said Marti.

"Well, what do you expect with the jet set?" countered Lila. "Clay was a business associate of Norton's. He told us all about it."

Marti's eyes, meeting Norton's, reflected sympathy. "I only met him once with Karen, but I thought he was terribly sweet. I'm sorry about what happened."

"So's he," said Norton. "I'm told you met Mr. Czardi in Hong Kong."

"That's right. I've been living there. I went there two years ago on a modeling job and liked it so much, I settled."

With whom, wondered Norton, loathing his awakening pang of jealousy. He cleared his throat nervously. "Stupid of me not to recognize you. I'm still using the deodorant you used to peddle on television."

"I wish others were," said Lila with a sly glance of distaste at Czardi.

Marti asked Norton, "Will you be in town long?"

"Hard to tell. Clay's death has left me a little up in the air. He was handling some business details for our company,

Brixton and Sons, which we were supposed to settle together. I'll have to retrace what he'd accomplished."

"How tiresome for you."

"But necessary."

The waiter arrived with Lila and Czardi's food. "What took you so long?" snapped Lila. "Did you have to go over to Chasen's to get it?" She lifted a gherkin and circumsized it with a ferocious bite.

"Are you hungry, Marti, darling?" asked Czardi, staring at his minute steak as though it had offended him.

"No, thank you. I had some scrambled eggs at home. How was the ballet?"

"As bad as this rotten sandwich," growled Lila through a mouthful of food. "The bacon's soggy, the chicken is tough, the tomatoes are tasteless, and, thank God, it's on the house." Norton thought of putting it on her head. Lila saw him staring at her food. "You want the rest of this? If you don't, I'm sending it over to the Board of Health."

"As a matter of fact, I'm famished." He moved the plate in front of him and dug in with relish, while Lila glowered at Czardi who chewed on a piece of steak with mincing movements of his mouth.

"Marti." Marti turned to Lila. "Is Karen very upset about Stopley?"

"Very."

"How's her black eye?" They stared at Norton. "That's quite a mouse she's got. She told me she fell off a horse in Palm Springs."

"Yes, she did," said Marti. "Karen'll never learn to sit a horse well. She'll never learn when to give them their head."

"Must have been tough on your photographer, posing her to keep that left eye hidden."

"He managed rather artistically, as a matter of fact."

And so are you, Marti, sweetheart, still lying as artistically as always. It's her right eye that took the punishment. You girls should have taken more time getting your stories straight. Norton popped the remainder of the sandwich into his mouth and munched away contentedly. He looked at his wristwatch and made a grimace.

"Are we keeping you up?" inquired Lila blandly.

"I've got a very early appointment. What time's the party tomorrow night?" Marti was staring inquisitively at Lila.

"From eight onwards." She gave him her address in Bel Air which he jotted down in his address book. "Pick me up around eight."

"Will do. Thanks for the hospitality, Mickey. And very nice meeting *you*, Miss Leigh. Well," he got to his feet, "me for the Doheny Dauphin." He was sure Marti got the message.

When he was out of earshot, Czardi leaned across the table to Lila in a rage. "Are you out of your mind taking him to Hagar's? She'll blow her top!"

"I'll blow yours if you don't lower your voice." She indicated the four dour-looking men at the adjoining table. "The Four Horsemen of the Apocalypse are all ears. Now use your head, you stupid hunky. I don't know if Mr. Valentine is for real or for wrong. Maybe he's legit and was being brought here by Stopley as a cover. But whatever, there's no keeping him from getting to Hagar's, and it's better if it's with me. If he's another snooper, I can keep a rein on him. I'll work it out with Hagar when I get home. Don't worry about it. It'll be a handpicked guest list. As a matter of fact, it'd be a good idea if the two of you were there."

Czardi was dripping with perspiration again as he hissed, "Wouldn't it be wiser if Hagar went to Mexico for a few weeks until this Stopley mess blows over?"

"It'll never blow over until the Feds are handed a killer. It was a stupid job in the first place, and we all know it. But it's too late now. We have to roll with the punches, and Hagar stays put. There's too much at stake. The old man wants to get back here, and the only way he can is when he can make a deal and write his own ticket. Now just relax, Mickey, and leave the driving to us. Now, Marti, *dar*ling, what the hell's this crap with Palm Springs and Karen's black eye?"

Norton made it back to the hotel without the Thunderbird escort. He undressed quickly, put on a robe, and mixed himself a nightcap. He turned out the living room lights and sat by the window staring out at the swimming pool. He welcomed Marti to his thoughts with open qualms. He wasn't kidding himself about still being in love with her. He was. It disgusted him to know she was sharing Czardi's bed. It frightened him that she was mixed up in the Hagar scene. She'd know soon enough how unsuccessful was her attempt to shore up Karen Frost's Palm Springs alibi. Karen must have been at Hagar's with Clay on Monday night. Marti could have been there too, with Czardi.

Marti couldn't have betrayed Clay. If she had, then she would have blown his own cover at the restaurant. Of course. She's protecting herself. She's in deep with this gang. How could she admit her ex-husband is a secret service man? Innocence be damned with vultures like these; they'd condemn her as guilty by past association. On the other hand, if she had fingered Clay, she could be spilling the beans about him right now.

Oh, Christ.

He began pacing the room. Did she or didn't she? Would she or wouldn't she? There was nothing in the manual to cover a situation like this. He sighed and sat down again. He'd have to play it by ear. Meet whatever emergency whenever it arose. But not like Clay. He would not let himself get cornered, beaten up and flung to his death. Marti heard him say Doheny Dauphin. She'll call. She'll be in touch somehow. Maybe she isn't fully aware of what she's gotten herself into. Czardi's probably just a way station for her, until someone better comes along. How the hell could she let that sweating pig touch her? *Count* Miklos Czardi. He reached for the phone, dialed, made a quick connection, spoke calmly and deliberately, spelling Czardi's name carefully, and then hung up. He took a swig of his drink when the phone rang.

"Valentine." He leaned back and listened. "I know. She tried to get a friend to back up her alibi, but it was bungled. No, I'll leave it alone for the time being. I've been invited to Mrs. Simon's tomorrow night. I'm escorting Lila Frank." He repeated the events of the evening. "Oh, I'm sure they're very suspicious of me by now. I've put immigration on to Czardi. He may be unimportant in this setup, but on the other hand, I recognized four fat paisanos in his place tonight." He listened for a while. "Yes, I'm well aware he fronts for them, but then, so do a few thousand others across the country. Most of them are in for a fee and nothing else. On the other hand, Czardi made a trip to Hong Kong last month, and we know what that could mean. By the way, he brought back a trophy with him." Norton exhaled and stared at the ceiling. "My ex-wife. She was the girl Czardi introduced me to tonight. No, she was rather good. She played dumb." He listened. "Well, I'll know soon enough if it was just for my benefit. Well, if she blows it, she blows it, and that's that. You replace me. I won't like it either. I think I can finish this job. They know killing Clay this close to home was an effing stupid mistake. I'll tell you this, I don't think his killing was planned. That's right. I think he just stumbled on something, and somebody ran scared, somebody who moves first and thinks afterward. I spoke to the coroner. There was dope in him but not that much alcohol. Probably acid. You know the kind of games they sometimes play at the castle. Clay probably joined in because it was expected of him. I'd do the same, except I'd use more caution about the dose. Come on, will you? You know what Clay was like." His face reddened with anger. "Then you should have waited until I was available to come out here and canceled him out! Oh, the hell with it! He's dead, right? I'm here, right? Do I continue, or do I go home? I can grab the first plane in the morning." He heard placating sounds from the receiver. "All right, then

I handle it my way." He listened again. "I'm sure I'll hear from Marti. The minute she thinks it's safe, I know I'll hear from her. By the way, there's a tail on me." He described the two men and their car. "They're very obvious, and it could be deliberate. They don't know I don't frighten easy." He listened and laughed and then hung up.

He stared at the phone he'd been talking into, loathing its turquoise color. Turquoise was Marti's favorite. The phone was a private one, not connected with the switchboard, installed before his arrival by prior arrangement. It was nothing unusual for the Doheny Dauphin. Most transients who did most of their work by telephone preferred a private instrument for outgoing calls. It was less expensive, and the hotel preferred it because it was less of a burden on the switchboard. Only the hotel, the telephone company and Norton's associates across the country knew of its existence and the private number.

While opting for a second nightcap, he wondered who had blackened Karen Frost's eye and why. Was it her dubious reward for the attempted bravery at defying an order? Maybe she'd really been hung up on Clay, knew the identity of his killer, demanded justice regardless of the consequences to herself. It would be nice to believe that, thought Norton. He had sampled some of her spirit and, in retrospect, admired it. Would he sample it again once she realized how tough a spot she was in? He hoped so. He needed her information. He needed information from all of them, either directly or by a slip of the tongue.

Hagar Simon's castle was a clearinghouse for evil. There had been and probably were setups similar to hers in London, Paris, Rome and God knows where else, possibly even in some remote outbacks missionaries hadn't heard of. Powerful men and distinguished careers were being deliberately and systematically broken to benefit one perfidious organization with a lust and greed for power unequaled since the pillaging and rampaging of the early Roman conquerors. And you couldn't pin a thing on Hagar. You couldn't subpoena her to testify before an investigating committee, because you weren't sure of what questions to ask. You knew that she frequently entertained financiers and politicians and statesmen and others of equal ilk who subsequently suffered scandal and ruin from which this one organization profited handsomely. The castle was known to be bugged and fitted with hidden cameras that recorded brief lapses in discretion brought about by a bevy of handpicked Loreleis who revered the almighty dollar above loyalty and patriotism. Norton's father, a distinguished Midwestern lawyer, had frequently reminded him: *Everybody has a price*. After his mother's death, his father told him with a tinge of acid humor, she occasionally extorted the price of a new dress or a new hat in return for sexual favors. He couldn't understand why his father paid. Norton had never found his mother the least bit attractive.

He couldn't finish the second drink. The last swig had almost made him gag. Old dauntless Norton was admitting to a twinge of fear. He was walking heavy-footed where angels feared to tread. He was pushing and pushing hard because murder overactivated his adrenalin. He was blockbusting because he had faith in his assessment of human frailty. Somewhere in this Hollywood setup, there was someone who could be frightened and intimidated into letting slip that one piece of information that could cause the entire evil structure to collapse.

Norton was jotting notes on a piece of hotel stationery. He was listing names and the potential they might offer him in his scheme of things. It was a form of game he played with himself because frequently he won. He had switched on a lamp, drawn the curtains, and left a cigarette he lit to smolder untouched in an ashtray, so deep was his concentration. Beside each name, he wrote the possible weakness he could play upon. Hagar Simon, Lila Frank, Miklos Czardi, Karen Frost, Chloe Jupiter, Viola Pickfair, Burton Hartley, and Marti. Unlike Abou Ben Adhem, Marti's name did not lead the rest. He wanted her to be an unimportant cog in the machinery, an innocent lamb among wolves. Even knowing her for what she had been and undoubtedly still was, he was still in love with her. It was seeing her that evening and feeling the old pang of jealousy that confirmed his feelings. So be it.

After four hours of troubled sleep, Norton awoke shortly before eight, shaved, showered, ordered breakfast and a newspaper. There was a three paragraph item about Clay on the lower, left-hand column on the third page. Murdered man found in Griffith Park. Nothing exotic enough about the killing to rate a headline. No severed head, no celebrity, just a solitary victim of murder, small pickings for this genocidal generation. Norton checked his horoscope, making a mental promise to himself to obey its injunctions to tidy up his house and find out why a friend was feeling ignored and then flung the papers on the couch. He hoped Viola Pickfair was an early riser. If she wasn't, she was about to be rudely awakened. He consulted his address book and dialed.

Viola Pickfair sounded as though she'd been up for hours wakening roosters. The voice was perky with bubbles and fizz and even adolescently petulant, as Norton heard, "I hope this is the exterminator because I can still hear that poor little mouse squealing in my woodwork and don't tell me I've got bats in my belfry because how can a little mouse survive in my woodwork after three days and if it got in there why isn't it smart enough to find its way out and oh my God there it goes again so what kind of an exterminator are you when I phoned you on Tuesday and here it is Thursday and I have to have my hair done . . ."

"Miss Pickfair!" Norton shouted.

"Speaking."

"This is *not* the exterminator."

"Then why are you calling?"

"My name is Norton Valentine. I . . ."

"*Norton*. You mean Norton who was standing in the hallway outside Karen's door last night talking to the ceiling 'Norton that was very poorly handled' or something like that

— 55 —

looking gorgeous in those blue jeans . . ."

She rambled on while he vaguely remembered a snub-nosed, raven-haired pixie wearing slacks and a see-through blouse.

". . . So you see I know who you are because Karen told me all about you and all about poor Clay and I think it's simply awful the way people are going around killing each other these days because somebody doesn't like the way they wear their hair or lovebeads or madras jackets . . ."

Bingo. The slip he'd been waiting for.

"Miss Pickfair?"

"Yes?"

"I wonder if I could pay you a visit this morning."

"Well I don't see why not," she said, sounding like Shirley Temple accepting an invitation to do a time-step with Bill Robinson, "but I don't see how I can be of much help to you because I only met Clay once and he barely said three words to me . . ."

Understandable, thought Norton, Boulder Dam wouldn't offer you a challenge.

". . . But if it'll make you think as though you're accomplishing something then come on right over because I live on . . ."

"I know where you live, Miss Pickfair. I got your name and address and phone number from Detective Sparks."

"Oh *him*." Her voice dropped several octaves and registered disgust. "What do you pal around with *him* for he's a drip he belongs in a bowling alley."

"What time would be convenient, Miss Pickfair?"

"*Viola*," she gurgled, "and I'll call you Norton because you sound like you belong in a book by Doctor Seuss and I always read a chapter of him before I go to bed with a cup of Ovaltine and a couple of Hydrox to nibble on and . . ."

"Why don't I come over now?"

"That'd be groovy and on the way do you mind stopping off and getting me a container of milk and some oranges and maybe a box of Fig Newtons . . ."

Thirty minutes later, carrying the bag of groceries, Norton stood on Viola Pickfair's threshhold. She lived in a ramshackle cottage on San Vincente just a few streets from his hotel. Viola held the door open staring at him with open disappointment.

"Awwwww you're not wearing your blue jeans." She wriggled to one side. "Come on in anyway because I like your open shirt it looks so sexy with that hair on your chest and here give me that bag and let's go into the kitchen because it's the cleanest and my purse is there and how much did all this cost and I hope you remembered to collect the green stamps because I'm saving up for a relaxercycle because Aunt Chloe says my bust needs developing . . ."

Norton swam with the stream of monologue into the kitchen, where she deposited the milk in the refrigerator and the other groceries on the shelf and then found her purse and meticulously counted out the coins with which to repay him. Counterpointing the business and the continuous flow of stream of consciousness, Norton studied the girl and decided that in repose, if ever, she would be an uncommonly beautiful little creature. She was barely five feet tall, and now with her hair in pigtails, wearing a man's shirt and pedal pushers, she resembled a backwoods gamin.

"I'll bet you think I'm cute," she said as though reading his mind.

"Very cute."

"Weeellll I'm older than you think but I won't tell you how much and I just made a fresh pot of coffee so let's have some okay?"

Once the coffee was poured and they sat around the small circular kitchen table, Viola appeared to have run out of steam and sat like a small child on her first day at school, waiting for Norton to make the next move. He took a sip of coffee, savored it, and said, "You make very good coffee."

"Thank you," she said, with a small voice, "and I'm really sorry about what happened to Clay. Karen told me you were good friends so I know how you must be feeling."

Norton folded his hands on the table. "Viola, why does everyone insist Clay wasn't at Hagar Simon's Monday night?"

"Because he wasn't that's why."

"How did you know he wore a madras jacket?"

"I didn't."

"On the phone you said something about people getting killed because of the way they wore their hair or love beads . . . or madras jackets."

"Norton two seconds after I've said it I don't remember what I've said . . . I just keep talking that's all because I guess I don't know how to stop . . . Does it drive you crazy too?"

He lied gracefully. "I think it's charming." She wrinkled her nose in appreciation. "But it just so happens that the night Clay was killed he was wearing a rented tuxedo with a madras jacket."

Her face sagged. "Oh."

"That's right, and so you can't blame me for wondering if perhaps you and a few others are perhaps lying as to whether Clay was at Mrs. Simon's that night."

"Well gee Norton I think somebody else was wearing a madras jacket that night. I mean they're not all that uncommon, are they? Let me think now I think it was maybe Burton Hartley . . . gee I really don't remember."

"Yes, I can see that's possible." She smiled gratefully. "What I don't understand is, if Clay *was* at Mrs. Simon's Monday night, why is everyone so anxious to insist he wasn't? After all, his body was found in Griffith Park. That's miles from Mrs. Simon's place."

"Well actually Norton though I went there with my Aunt Chloe I didn't stay very long because I had a date with a friend of mine so maybe if he was there he arrived after I left . . . Doesn't that make sense?"

He felt she was asking herself the question. "There's no arguing that."

"Oh good."

"Karen Frost's a good friend of yours, isn't she?"

"Oh yeah . . . she introduces me to all the producers and directors and casting agents she knows because she doesn't feel any rivalry the way other women do and she knows and so does everybody else know I don't want to get ahead on my Aunt Chloe's reputation which is why I changed my name from Selma O'Flaherty to Viola Pickfair . . . Viola is my favorite instrument and Pickfair is where Mary Pickford lives with Buddy Rogers her husband who supplanted in her affections the late Douglas Fairbanks Senior who first lived at Pickfair with Mary . . ."

"Who socked Karen in the eye?"

"She fell off a horse."

"In Palm Springs."

"That's right . . . Palm Springs."

"She was there on a job with Marti Leigh."

"She was?" Norton smiled gently. "That's right! She was there with Marti Leigh!"

"Viola."

"Yes?" she said meekly.

"I think it's all a trumped up story." Viola appeared to be on the verge of tears. "I think Karen knows more about Clay's murder than she dares to tell, and somebody socked her in the eye as a warning."

There was a catch in Viola's voice, as she insisted, "Honest Karen's a wonderful girl . . . she adored Clay she really did. She's all broken up about it . . . I mean after you left her she just cried and cried and gee it made her eye look even worse."

"Were you there when she phoned Marti Leigh?"

"No," came the swift response, "she phoned her after I left."

"How do you know?"

"How do I know?"

"How do you know?"

"Because . . ." she stared at the stove for a moment before continuing ". . . because I called her before I went to bed to see if she was feeling better and she said she was feeling better because she had talked to Marti who was very sympathetic and told her to bathe her eye and get a good night's sleep and not to take too many sleeping pills because they could make her sick."

"Or dead."

"Oh don't say *that!*"

"Viola, are you really all this naive?"

She pushed her cup and saucer to one side and was a picture of infinite sadness. "Norton my Aunt Chloe says I'm so dumb she can't understand why I'm not a star by now. I'm going to be thirty years old soon Norton and it's getting a little late . . . So now I go to school every day to learn shorthand and typing."

"I think that's very wise of you, Viola." Then he added, "Are you invited to Mrs. Simon's often?"

"Oh no . . . Monday was my first . . . I just begged and begged Aunt Chloe to take me with her . . . Aunt Chloe doesn't like to go there ever but she does from time to time because they're neighbors and it isn't neighborly to refuse too many invitations even if she can't stand Hagar . . . oh that isn't what I mean . . . what I mean is . . ."

"Don't explain it," said Norton reaching over to pat her hand, "maybe you did leave before Clay arrived."

"Norton?"

"Yes?"

"Are you really a stockbroker?"

He crossed his legs. "Who says I'm not?"

"You don't ask questions like a stockbroker. Karen says maybe Clay wasn't a stockbroker either . . . I have to get ready to go to school." She pushed her chair back and began to tidy up the kitchen table.

"I want you to do me a favor, Viola."

"Well if I can sure." She was filling the sink with water and detergent into which she placed the cups and saucers.

"I'd appreciate your calling your Aunt Chloe and asking her to let me come visit her."

"And ask more questions?"

"She was my favorite movie star. I used to have her picture taped to the inside of my gymnasium locker when I was a kid at school."

"If she'll see you don't tell her how many years ago that was."

"Would you call her?"

Viola thought for a moment, then sighed, and said, "Okay." She turned off the water tap and disappeared into the living room. Norton left his chair and stared out a window into Viola's backyard. There wàs a child's swing, a sandbox and an overgrowth of weeds. Viola the child-woman forced to play adult games. Tossed by chance into a cesspool situation. Instructed to lie but not even good enough an actress to carry that off. Maybe Monday was her first night at Hagar Simon's. Maybe she really hadn't seen Clay there. Maybe I'm kidding myself and she's actually a better actress than all of them. But there were too many slips. Too many delicious slips. The madras jacket. The black eye. Palm Springs. Marti.

"Aunt Chloe says you can come over in an hour."

He hadn't heard her return and then realized why. She had removed her shoes. "Thanks a lot, Viola. I appreciate this." Then, like a whirlwind, she rushed across the room and threw her arms around him, pressing her cheek tightly against his bared chest.

"It's only fifteen minutes from here to Aunt Chloe's which gives us plenty of time for a quick one what do you say Norton I really dig you the most!"

Some child-woman.

Very gently, he pried her loose from him and cupped her face in his hands and looked into her hungry little eyes. He bent his head and kissed her hotly while his tongue pried her mouth open and counted her teeth. Then he whispered gently, "I'll try to send the rest over later."

"You fink!" she snarled, and went stomping to the front door, pulling it open for him. "You won't get anything out of Aunt Chloe either! She just wants to see what you look like!"

"Thanks for the coffee and the kiss." She stared at him

dumbly with disappointment and a childish pout. "And Viola, try to keep away from bad company."

"Oh get out of here!"

He stepped out to the front porch and headed down the stairs while Viola stood in the doorway biting on a thumb. He turned and waved, and she quickly shut the door. Norton got into the Renault and pulled away to Santa Monica Boulevard. Through the rearview mirror, he saw the white Thunderbird pull out of a hidden driveway and follow him. He resisted the urge to tootle his horn in greeting.

5

Norton spent an exhilarating hour leading the white Thunderbird on a tour of Hollywood. He had started the morning with a full tank and hoped they hadn't. He flirted with traffic violations by jumping lights and making turns from the wrong lanes, but the boys on his tail kept right with him. He was tempted to pick up a hitchhiker on Wilshire Boulevard, but from the leer on the boy's face, he could guess his desired destination was the nearest bedroom for a modest fee. At precisely one hour from the time he left Viola Pickfair's cottage, Norton passed Hagar Simon's castle and pulled into Chloe Jupiter's driveway. He saw the Thunderbird slow down and settle across the road from Chloe's under a shade tree. In the glare of a blazing sun, the heart-shaped house resembled an expensive French dessert. Norton took the steps leading to the front door two at a time, pressed the bell, and heard the chimes tinkling the opening bars of "Bewitched, Bothered and Bewildered."

After what seemed like an interminable wait, Norton was about to press the bell again when the door slowly opened. Norton was staggered by the sight confronting him. He saw an abnormally tall, powerfully built black man, naked except for a brief leopard-skin loincloth. His huge frame almost filled the doorway, and Norton felt it would take more than a battering ram to get past him.

"Oh . . . er . . . hi! Good morning. I'm Norton Valentine. I believe Miss Jupiter is expecting me."

"Good morning, Mr. Valentine. Won't you come in?" The voice was beautifully modulated and cultured. "I am Horace X., Miss Jupiter's butler. The reception room is through the heart-shaped entrance at your right." He closed the door and followed Norton to the reception room. The hallway into which Norton had entered was decorated with nymphs, fauns and cherubs. The floor was Italian marble, and from the ceiling, there hung a chandelier with heart-shaped bulbs. The reception room was even more titillating. The walls were embossed with a series of frescoes depicting satyrs and naked victims in a variety of scenes and positions that could have brought on heart attacks to the most hardened censors. The sofa and easy chairs were upholstered in ermine, and everything else was heart-shaped, from the coffee tables and end tables to a white piano that, of course, boasted a white, heart-shaped stool.

"Ostentatious," commented Horace X. solemnly, "but we call it home. May I pour you a drink? My Bloody Marys are legend."

"What will Miss Jupiter be drinking?"

"Imported mineral water. Miss Jupiter neither touches alcohol nor uses tobacco. She is a very religious woman."

"I'll have a Bloody Mary." Horace X. looked pleased, as he crossed to the bar near the piano and began mixing the drink.

"Do forgive my attire," said the butler, as he measured the vodka into a heart-shaped pitcher. "I've been posing for Miss Jupiter."

"She paints?"

"Sculpts."

"Sorry to interrupt."

"I'm grateful. I've been carrying the world on my shoul-

— 64 —

ders for the past two hours." He looked at Norton with an impish grin. "Miss Jupiter never suffers an energy crisis."

"Don't brag, Horace," Norton heard from behind him. "Just mix the drink." Norton turned and saw the fabulous lady entering through a panel in the wall that slid shut behind her. She advanced slowly, hands delicately placed on her hips, blazing red hair crowned by a glittering tiara, a diaphanous gown carefully tailored to accentuate every curve of her amazingly youthful-looking body, the hips undulating as he had seen them undulate in dozens of films. Her skin was unlined ivory, and though the eyes were heavily made up, there was but a trace of orange lipstick. She wasn't much taller than her niece, yet gave the impression of a statuesque beauty. Though she looked years younger, Norton knew she was old enough to be his mother and was glad she wasn't. She stopped a few feet away from him and slowly surveyed him from head to toe, like an art expert examining a potential purchase.

"Ummmm, uh, Norton, . . . uh hope the neighbors saw yuh comin' up the driveway. . . . It might change muh image around here." Norton couldn't find his voice but managed his stupid grin. Her eyes studied his face again and then slowly traveled downward. "Ummmmmuh, Norton, . . . uh see you're not unarmed." He blushed while she smiled the famous smile that bespoke a private joke. "Yuh look nervous, Norton. Would you like a tranquilizer, honey?"

He found his voice. "I guess I'm a bit overwhelmed, Miss Jupiter."

"Why, of course yuh are, Norton. Uh sympathize. Sit over there in the easy chair, Norton, and take it easy. Uh'll sit over here right across from yuh an' continue feastin'. Hurry up with them drinks, Horace."

"Coming right up."

"Uh hope yuh mean the drinks." She smiled at Norton, who was trying to look comfortable and at ease. "Viola tells me yuh one of muh fans. Is this a business call or a pilgrimage?"

Norton cleared his throat. "A mixture of both, I guess."
Horace X. served the drinks and then departed.

"Well, uh hope yuh not in too much of a hurry. Uh like tuh get tuh know people first, if yuh know what uh mean."

"Yes. Sure." Nervously, he took a sip of the Bloody Mary. "Wow. This is quite a drink."

"Uh only serve the best of everything." She positioned herself provocatively, ignoring the heart-shaped glass of mineral water on the table next to her easy chair. "Horace is quite a boy. Uh discovered him on a television show. Uh was watchin' the Watts riots and saw him arrested. Uh bailed him out and brought him home. Finders, keepers."

"He's a treasure."

"Howdja guess? Well, tell me, Norton, how do uh look tuh yuh?"

"Sensational."

She smiled with pleasure. "And uh ain't had no face lifts or nothin' else lifted, and uh got genyoowine medical certificates tuh prove it. Yuh know how uh keep muh figgah, muh youth, muh beauty, muh sexual appeal? Well uh'm gonna tell yuh. First of all, uh don't touch spirits and uh don't use tobacco. Second of all, uh get twelve hours of sleep on . . . ummmmm . . . certain nights of the week. Third of all, uh read muh bible one hour every mornin', and one hour every night, regardless of who uh'm entertainin'. And fourth, uh only eat organic foods, yuh know, grown by muh puhsonal organics. Yuh look like yuh had a bad night, Norton. Anyone worthwhile?"

Norton sat forward, holding the glass with both hands. "I think you know why I'm here, Miss Jupiter."

"Oh, uh do? Somebody tell yuh uh also read minds?"

Norton smiled. "I think on occasion you know how to read minds."

"Yeah, and uh hope uh don't have tuh take soap and water tuh yours." She reached for her mineral water and took a sip. "This is bottled special for me, by some monks in a monastery in Switzerland." Her eyes twinkled as she set the glass back on the table. "Uh drove most of 'em there. A woman what lives by the Bible, Norton, don't like lyin'. But yuh see, Norton, like a lotta works of art, uh'm a flawed masterpiece. Uh know what yuh're after. It's this Clay Stopley business. Uh read the piece on him in the *Times* this mornin'. Not much of a piece, was it? He should fire his press agent." She slowly wriggled to her feet and paced the floor. Norton now realized she was wearing platform shoes. "Uh mean uh already said muh piece to that detective man, Sparks." She stopped in front of Norton and stared down at him. "Uh like yuh looks better. Yuh're Ivy League, uh can tell. Uh gotta green thumb. Uh suppose yuh wonderin' if uh'm tryin' tuh protect Hagar just because we're neighbors. Well, uh ain't." She resumed her slow, measured pacing. "Uh don't much like Hagar, and uh told Isaac he was a fool tuh marry her. Why, when he first introduced me tuh her, she was so dumb, she was confused by indoor plumbin'. Of course, she's learned a lot since then. But, yuh see, she still lives in the past. She's still readin' *Anthony Adverse*.

"Uh don't make no bones about muh age. Uh'm proud of it and the fact uh don't look it. That's because uh live for today. Uh move along with the times. That's why, every generation, uh win a million new fans. The kids today worship me the way their fathers and, yeah, their grandfathers did. Uh mean there's one old beau of mine uh visit every week in the veteran's hospital what still remembers my theatrical dayboo in *The Mikado*."

"Really?" said Norton. "What part did you play?"

"Well, whaddya think?" she said, sauntering toward him slowly then stopping a few inches from his face and gently grinding her hips. "Yum Yum."

The effect was too much for Norton. He burst into laughter, and after a beat, she joined in with him.

"Norton, uh really think uh like yuh. Yuh can tell when uh'm puttin' yuh on. Yuh know, muh career's the biggest put-on in show business history. Of course, uh'm enjoyin' the joke more than anybody else. Uh mean, uh'm glad yuh know uh ain't tryin' to seduce yuh. Not yet. Of course, tuh kiss muh lips is like touchin' the third rail." She was now posed against the piano, her left hand resting on the piano, her right hand gently caressing her hair. "Now, murder is a serious business. Uh don't hold with all this killin' goin' on in the world. President Kennedy, his brother, Martin Luther King. Uh mean, it's indecent, and if yuh been followin' muh long and respected career like yuh say yuh do, then yuh know uh ain't never done nothin' indecent in muh entire life." She appeared to be giving that statement further thought. "Uh mean, if uh did," she said with a sly smile, "uh made sure uh never got caught." She headed back to her seat and the mineral water and while carefully lowering herself, said, "Uh mean, uh'm shuah yuh know uh ain't anybody's fool. Uh got a very good mind. Uh once exchanged theories of relativity with Albert Einstein. Mmmmuhhh . . . he liked mine better."

Norton was on his feet, crossing to the bar with his empty glass. "Miss Jupiter, the newspapers omitted to mention how Clay Stopley was killed. He'd been badly beaten, and just about every bone in his body was broken." She clucked her tongue. "The police assume he was thrown from a great height . . . or perhaps possibly crushed to death. Er . . . I believe, somewhere on your premises, you keep a gorilla named Irving?"

Her face hardened. "Are yuh insinuatin' Irvin' would crush a man in his arms?" She stuck out her chin and said with indignation, "Why, muh Irvin' ain't no pansy!" She got to her feet with youthful vigor. "Why, muh Irvin' is what the Spanish call real *macho*. Irvin' is all man, exceptin' he's a gorilla." She was crossing to the wall panel through which she had entered. "Uh want yuh to meet Irvin' and see for yuhself." Norton paled as she pressed a hidden spring in the wall that released the panel. It slid back slowly. "Irvin'!" she shouted. "Turn off that 'Love Of Life' and come in here. Uh want yuh tuh meet a friend of mine." She slowly sauntered back to her chair and sat while Norton stood transfixed with eyes glued to the opening in the wall.

The gorilla entered slowly, wet eyes blinking. Irving and Norton examined each other with equal interest. "Come over here, Irvin'," commanded Chloe, "and crouch at muh feet. Come on over here, Norton, and shake hands with Irvin'." As the gorilla settled in position at Chloe's feet, Norton slowly moved forward. "Well, come on, Norton," said Chloe impatiently, "he ain't gonna hurt yuh. Irvin' is a lamb. Uh've had him since he was a pup. He's been tutored by some of the best teachers money can buy. He's got a higher I.Q. than any William Morris agent. D'yuh know Princeton College is beggin' for his brain when he dies? Uh won't give 'em no commitment unless they offer him first a honorary degree. Now don't be coy, Irvin', and shake Norton's hand. He's muh friend. He's got class, can'tcha tell?"

Gently, the gorilla took Norton's hand in his own and shook it.

"Now how about *that!*" exclaimed Chloe triumphantly to Norton. "Was that the grip of a killer? Besides, he's got a alibi for Monday night. He was here with Horace X. and Horace's mother Louella—she's muh puhsonal maid—watchin' television. Irvin' never misses 'M.A.S.H.'" Irving's eyes brightened. "Uh don't understand it m'self, but he's nuts about Alan Alda. Go ahead, Norton, if yuh wanna question Irvin'. Well, don't look so dumb. He understands English. Uh told yuh he was smart. Why, when some of muh friends come over for a friendly game of charades, everybody fights tuh get Irvin' on their team."

Norton could feel the perspiration trickling down his back. It was too bizarre, too weird, too unreal for him. He actually believed he saw a smug expression on Irving as the gorilla blithely examined a fingernail. "I . . . er . . . don't doubt that he has an alibi."

"Why, of course, he has an alibi. Uh told yuh before, uh live by the good book. All right Irvin', yuh can go back tuh the television set and shut the panel behind you."

The gorilla extended a hand to Norton once again. Norton shook it, while Chloe beamed with pride. "Irvin' likes yuh. That's a very favorable sign, Norton. Irvin' can spot a phony faster than he can find a flea." The gorilla was gone, and the panel slid shut. "Now, who made them insinuations against muh Irvin'?"

"Detective Sparks. May I pour myself another drink?"

"Why, shuah, honey, yuh look like yuh could use some coolin' off. Irvin's your friend now. Yuh got nothin' to worry about. Why, some night if yuh free and Irvin's free, yuh drop by and take him out for a pizza and a movie, especially if it's somethin' with Faye Dunaway. The only time he ever walked out on her was *The Eyes of Laura Mars*. And listen, Norton, from now on yuh can call me Chloe. Yuh Irvin's friend, and yuh my friend, so uh'm gonna give yuh a piece of advice. Pack yuh bags and go home, and leave this investigation to the police."

Norton stared at her from the bar. "Is that friendly advice or a warning?"

She replied softly and with sincerity, "It's both. Yuh gettin' in over yuh head. Uh watched yuh drivin' up from muh boodwah. I saw yuh was bein' trailed. I recognized them two hoods in the Thunderbird. I was watchin' through muh platinum field glasses. When them two hoods are on yuh trail, that means somebody means business."

"So do I." He sipped his drink and looked at the woman over the rim of his glass. He was pleased with the expression of admiration he saw. He liked Chloe Jupiter, and he respected her. She was indeed nobody's fool and undoubtedly a very brave woman. He could understand now that Horace X. and Irving weren't in residence for the camp effect. They were her bodyguards and possibly on the vanguard of a retinue situated in other parts of the house.

"Viola says yuh say yuh're a stockbroker. Well, Viola's got a brain yuh could pick up with a pin. Who are yuh, handsome? What's yuh real name?"

"Norton Valentine's my real name."

"Well, yuh'll have tuh change it for movin' pitchers."

"And I know I can trust you."

"Yuh better believe it," she said warmly.

"I'm a government investigator. A secret service man."

"Ohhhhh?" Her eyes blazed with renewed interest. "Uh got some secrets yuh could service."

He sat down opposite her. "Clay Stopley was here on a top secret assignment. He slipped up, and he's dead."

She said seriously, "Well, don't yuh go slippin' up."

"I'll do my best not to. Now tell me the truth, *was* Clay at Hagar Simon's Monday night?"

"Ain't yuh afraid muh place is bugged?"

"Is it?"

She smiled slowly. "Yuh know it ain't. Nobody can sneak past my boys."

"What about it. Was Clay there?"

"Yuh muh friend, right?"

"Very right."

"He was there, but yuh didn't hear it from me, right?"

"Chloe Jupiter, I am going to kiss you!"

"Yuh better leave yuh drink on the table, unless yuh like it pipin' hot." He left the drink and his chair and kissed her. "It'll do for now. Now sit down, and yuh listen tuh me, and yuh listen good."

Norton returned to his easy chair and listened. "Uh want yuh tuh understand uh ain't deliberately rattin' on anybody. Yuh see uh'm not all that sure what's really goin' on at Hagar's besides her providin' amusement for a lot of visitin' bigwigs. Now, uh don't like tuh see yuh lookin' so skeptical. Uh know yuh know uh wasn't born yesterday, but uh want yuh to know uh'm like them three Chinese monkeys what don't speak, hear, or see no evil. So just keep yuh face in neutral and listen. Just remember in the old days when uh spoke muh piece, even Clark Gable was all ears. Uh been puttin' two and two t'gether while we been banterin' here.

Yuh friend was found in Griffith Park, but yuh think he mighta been killed at Hagar's, right?"

"Yes."

"Well, if it's so, then it's not only a sin and illegal, it's immoral." She paused and regarded Norton solemnly. "Uh also had Viola there with me, which was muh second mistake. The first was muh own presence, but uh'll explain the reason for that later. Uh came early, and uh left early, right after dinner, and that's the truth. But when uh left, the last uh saw of yuh friend Stopley, he was sandwiched on a love seat between that Karen Frost and another beauty whose name uh never caught."

The muscles tensed in Norton's face. Chloe had now given him two valuable pieces of information. Clay Stopley had definitely been a guest of Hagar Simon on Monday night, and Karen Frost had lied to him, undoubtedly thanks to her blackened eye. Could the other girl have been Marti? "Was any pot being passed around?"

"Why should there?" asked Chloe with a perplexed look, "Hagar's got plenty of terlets."

Norton swallowed a laugh with effort. "Pot's another word for marijuana."

Chloe smiled slyly. "Uh know that, handsome. But uh can't resist a good crack. Shuah, there was pot bein' passed around. That's why uh left. Uh didn't exit laughin' either. Viola wouldn't leave with me. It took a lot of coaxin' on her part tuh get me tuh take her with me in the first place. But youth is so headstrong and impulsive." She made lazy circles in the air with her wrists. "So uh let her have it with both barrels in the privacy of the front hall and then left her there. Uh can tell by yuh face she lied to yuh about that."

Norton nodded. "She lied."

"She gets that from her father's side." She pursed her lips and stared at the piano. "Uh'll have a talk with her later and see what she knows. Yuh leave her to me. Now this wasn't one of Hagar's big parties. It was sort of a intimate group, maybe about ten or so, set up for this here Jap . . ."

"Udo Yosaka."

"Yeah, that's him. Not bad lookin' for a Oriental. Now, yuh know uh ain't got no racial prejudices, but while so help me uh'm too young tuh remember the *Maine*, uh sure won't forget Pearl Harbor, so uh couldn't bring muhself tuh be witty and entertain' for the gentleman. Uh also know from past experience the pot was only an appetizer, and while Hagar ain't never been busted, uh ain't one tuh tempt the fates, so uh took muh leave. Uh could use a little of muh mineral water, handsome."

Norton reached for her glass and went to the bar to refill it. He felt lightheaded, and there was a new spring in his step. He was feeling like a slot-machine player hitting the jackpot with his first fifty-cent piece. But, like the player, he was beginning to wonder why it was all so easy, why luck was so suddenly on his side. Was Chloe Jupiter truly on the square, or had she been primed for this interview? There had been an hour between Viola's phone call to her aunt and Norton's arrival for the privileged audience, more than enough time for Chloe to contact the right person or persons and agree on her response. He didn't want to believe that. In any investigation, he was trained to be alert, cautious, and to exercise suspicion, but in Chloe's case, there was one item that caused him to believe she was being genuinely cooperative: the revelation that Karen Frost had been at the castle Monday night. And Norton was convinced that Karen had been intimidated and threatened because she knew or suspected the identity of Clay's killer. He returned to Chloe with the glass of mineral water and realized she had spent the past minute quietly studying him and reading his mind again.

"Yuh wonderin' whether or not tuh trust me," she said, taking the glass from Norton.

"I'm obliged to. It's part of my job."

"Uh got a puhsonal reason for levelin' with yuh, because it has tuh do with muh religious beliefs. It's the commandment that says, 'Thou shalt not kill.' And murder can become a contagious disease. Yuh see uh thought a long time ago

— 73 —

things would start gettin' too hot over at Hagar's. Like when uh warned her years ago not to play Joan of Arc on skates, even though the chances were the last part of the pitcher would sizzle. So uh told her recently, 'Hagar, when things start to come tuh a boil, yuh ain't gonna be able to manufactcher enough ice tuh cool it down.' Now there's been a murder, and things are gettin' hot. Uh'm hopin' what little uh tell yuh will help yuh and yuh department to prevent further bloodshed. And uh'm worried about Viola. The little twerp's been lyin' tuh me too, and uh gotta protect her, look after her. Uh promised her mother, muh sister Angie, on her deathbed that uh'd look after Viola like she was muh own child. And like she was muh own child," her voice rose in fury, "uh'm gonna paddle her backside until it's red enough to stop traffic."

Chloe resumed pacing like a troubled Cassandra, hands on hips and the tiara in her hair trembling like a television antenna in a strong wind. "Uh'll tell yuh this much, whoever the brains are behind all this, uh don't think it's Hagar. Uh'm shuah it's obvious tuh yuh she's gettin' paid a packet tuh front these here dinners and parties of hers."

"We know her husband died a bankrupt." He told Chloe about his conversation with Lila Frank flying over Colorado and how, through the assistance of such friends as Harvey Tripp, Hagar had presumably since made some shrewd and profitable investments.

Chloe fed the information to her built-in computer and then commented, "Mebbe so, and if it's so, then Hagar's a damned fool not tuh get out."

"I think she's in too deep, even if she wanted to."

"Then may God have mercy on her, but uh got no sympathy for anybody what's got blood on their hands. Norton, uh been givin' yuh a lot of cooperation here. Now uh want a little from yuh."

"Ask away."

"Uh want yuh tuh promise to help keep Viola in the clear." He started to speak and she raised her hand. "Don't interrupt. Uh'm shuah muh niece was just an innocent bystander that night. Uh mean, uh know she's too dumb to be more than that. Damn it, what uh'm trying' tuh tell yuh is, if yuh can do it, keep her name outta the papers. It's gonna be tough enough tryin' tuh keep muh own out when the time comes." She smiled at Norton. "Uh know when the mud hits the fan, muh name is bound to come up. Uh been tuh so many of her swah-rays. But that was as a favor to a old business associate." She took a deep breath. "Yuh know uh owed muh break in pitchers to Isaac Simon. He took a chance on me when nobody else would. The other studios at the time said uh was too much like muh friend Mae West. Well, neither Mae or me could see the similarity, and for that matter, neither could Isaac. So he put me in that pitcher with his own money. Yuh remember *Queen For A Knight?*"

"I sure do!" acknowledged Norton with gusto.

"Yeah, that was some pitcher. Why when uh sang 'North Pole Papa, Uh Hope You're Goin' South Tonight,' uh not only made screen history, uh got some two hundred theatre managers across the country jailed for impairin' the public morals." She turned to Norton and pointed a finger at him. "It's about then uh turned to religion and started readin' muh Bible. Uh got lotsa favorites in the Old Testament. Like Shadrach, Meshach and ToBedWeGo." She was at Norton's side with a friendly hand on his shoulder. "Now yuh leave Viola tuh me. If she knows anythin' and gives me any trouble about spillin' it, then uh'll get Irvin' tuh squeeze it out of her." Her eyes met Norton's. "Gently, of course. Yuh can believe it when uh tell yuh Irvin' ain't no bone crusher. He's too refeened. Now, Norton, don't take this too puhsonal, but uh'm gonna ask yuh tuh take yuh leave right now." She led the way to the door. "Uh'm a little tired, and uh need muh rest. Now, uh want yuh to write down muh private number and call me anytime yuh feel yuh need tuh talk tuh me, or anythin' else that might come tuh mind." He couldn't see her face, but he imagined she was smiling slyly. She turned slightly and saw he had his address book open with pen poised to write and gave him her private telephone number. As though having received a telepathic message, Horace X., now properly attired in a butler's uniform decorated with hearts, stood holding the front door open. Chloe raised her right hand, and Norton took it and kissed it. Chloe beamed with pleasure.

"I believe in you, Chloe," said Norton, "and I can't thank you enough."

"That's right, yuh can't." She patted him on the back, and he left. Chloe sauntered toward the rear of the house and shouted, *"Louella!* Peel me a kumquat, and bring me muh Proust!"

Norton's Renault shot past the Thunderbird. He leaned out the window and shouted, "Back to my hotel, men!"

The thug with the curly red hair muttered an oath, while his blond confederate dog-eared a comic book and settled back for the chase.

No artist had ever succeeded in capturing on canvas the cool madonnalike beauty of Hagar Simon. There hung in the drawing room of Hagar's private second-floor suite an early painting of her by Anagoni. It caught an icy aloofness, the artist undoubtedly subconsciously influenced by her prowess with skates. But the subtle sadness of her amber eyes, detected on past occasions by a few devoted friends who had since passed out of her life, had escaped even this celebrated Italian master. Reclining on a chaise on the balcony that extended cantilevered from her bedroom, the middle-aged beauty's face reflected a haunting unhappiness. It recalled the fairy-tale heroine Rapunzel, trapped in her tower, awaiting a call from below from her lover: "Rapunzel, Rapunzel, let down your long hair!"

On Hagar's lap was a paper pad, and in her right hand she loosely held a gold fountain pen. The pad was open to a sheet of paper on which there was a guest list. She was staring into the distance at the two retreating automobiles, the Renault and the white Thunderbird. Then her eyes moved slowly to Chloe Jupiter's pastry of a house. Hagar's sigh was colored by a heaviness of heart and a nagging feeling of misgiving and apprehension that worried her nerves like the agonizing pain of a terminal disease.

She found herself of late dwelling on the memory of her respected, albeit unloved, husband Isaac. Isaac had taught her to face the world bravely and with dignity and to ignore the cruel jokes at the expense of her almost nonexistent acting ability. He made her believe in herself as something more than an entertaining novelty who could perform a flawless figure eight and do a breathtaking flying leap through six carefully-spaced burning hoops with a split-second timing that defied the danger of self-immolation. Although now edging fifty, Hagar could still perform an effortless figure eight, still jumped through hoops, and still worried about the hazardous flames.

"Say, what the hell's bothering you?" rasped Lila Frank, studying Hagar from the entrance to the bedroom. Her right hand was choking the neck of a bottle of beer. The other hand held a ham sandwich as though she'd been using it to dust the furniture. She wolfed a bite of sandwich while settling cross-legged on a leather-covered hassock.

"I just saw the boys hot in pursuit of Mr. Valentine. He's been visiting with Chloe." As Hagar spoke, she dropped the fountain pen on a wicker table and placed her hand over the guest list, her tapering lacquered nails resembling organ stops. "Chloe's angry with me. She hasn't forgiven me for urging Viola to remain at the party after Chloe decided to leave. Now Viola's implicated, and Chloe's furious. She came by after lunch yesterday in her coach and four and let me have it in what could hardly be called uncertain terms. She brought the gorilla, and he terrifies the life out of me." She glared at Lila. "I want to go away." Lila continued ruminating thoughtfully. "After tonight's party, I want to go away. I'm not well. You know I'm not well. I need a rest. The doctor has warned me, I can't continue this pace."

"I'm warning you, you have to," said Lila harshly. "I wouldn't let your doctor treat a blister."

"I'm not at all well," resumed Hagar, as though Lila hadn't spoken. "The condition of my heart is worsening. I need an operation." Lila flung the remains of her sandwich over the iron railing and took a swig of beer. "If I don't have it soon, I might not see another Christmas."

"Does the boyfriend know this?"

"No, he doesn't, and he's not going to." The threat in Hagar's voice didn't escape Lila. "What happened Monday night seriously aggravated my condition."

"It's aggravated a lot of conditions!" snapped Lila. She rubbed the beer bottle against her brow, while lost in thought.

"I'm of no use anymore," said Hagar. "I'm tired. I'm spent. I'm not clever. It would be better for all of us if I lost myself somewhere."

"You weren't by any chance thinking of Italy?" Lila looked and sounded fiendish.

"No, you bitch, I wasn't thinking of Italy. That was finished years ago."

"It's *never* finished!" hammered Lila.

Hagar flung the paper pad aside with a violent gesture. "Well, it's goddamned well going to be finished!"

Lila pointed the beer bottle at Hagar threateningly. "Don't you use that tone of voice with me. You're in so deep a submarine couldn't reach you! *What* heart? Who you jazzing? Me? Lila?" She leapt to her feet and looked down at Hagar menacingly. "You think we don't know the amount of funds you've been transferring to Rio? We know *everything!*"

"So *what!* I earned every nickel of it, and I'll do as I please with it!" She made a dramatically sweeping gesture. "This operation is finished! Stopley's murder did that! Don't look at me as though I'm betraying you! The government's on to us, and God knows what they know by now!"

"They don't know nothing!" Lila slammed the beer bottle

on the wicker table and crossed to the guard railing, leaning against it with her arms folded, surveying Hagar with a contempt she usually reserved for a dilatory servant. "You most certainly are not clever, Hagar. What the hell did the old man ever see in you?"

"He couldn't have Chloe. I was second best. And he's got no complaint. I've done my job well. I'm too old for the pill, and I'm too young for social security, and I'm not asking for a pension or a gold watch for faithful service, but I'm owed this much: the right to get away while there's still time."

Lila stared at the sky and entreated, "Mother of Mercy, how do I tell this Snow Queen she's got nothing to worry about? How do I tell her Norton Valentine is going to end up chasing his own tail? How, Mother, how do I tell her?"

"How do you know Chloe hasn't told him Stopley was here Monday night?"

"She wouldn't."

"How do you know?"

"Because she owes the old man too much."

"You can't scare Chloe, you know that."

"Chloe wouldn't grass."

"I wouldn't be so sure. You didn't see what she was like when she came to see me yesterday. She didn't like what's happened with Viola. She didn't like being interrogated by Sparks. She doesn't like the idea of adverse publicity of any sort. And that gorilla of hers refused a banana." Hagar was on her feet and moving slowly toward the bedroom. She lifted her eyes to a rampart overhead and shuddered. Then she turned, and her eyes met Lila's. "Mr. Valentine has you worried, doesn't he?"

"Any snooper does."

"You tell me he's smart. Much smarter than Mr. Stopley."

"Much."

"In less than twenty-four hours, he's gotten to you, to Karen, to Mickey and Marti, Viola, Chloe . . . and tonight he'll be here."

"Where the trail goes cold."

"You hope."

"I know."

"You don't know enough Lila. Trying to frighten him off with those muscle men isn't working."

"It's getting on his nerves. I could see that last night at Czardi's."

"He probably saw more."

"Now *you're* getting on *my* nerves."

"I'm glad to see you still have some left."

Lila moved forward slowly. "I don't like you, Hagar."

"Tell me something new."

"I never trusted you, and now I trust you less."

Hagar smiled coldly. "But you're stuck with me. You can't do a thing to me. Not even murder." The women were now face to face, and Hagar gently, mockingly, patted Lila's cheek. "I've transferred much more than funds to Rio, Lila. If I go, you all go with me." Lila's face belonged in a poker game. "I'm sure when I told you about my heart, you were surprised to hear I had one. Well, I'm not lying. I'm not copping a phony plea. I am a very sick woman. I need this surgery, and it can't be delayed too long. I would like to leave within a few days. I shall somehow weather this charade you've foisted on me this evening for Mr. Valentine's benefit, which is as pointless a gesture as attempting to frighten him away from his investigation. Federal investigators proliferate like babies in a Catholic family. I think you should contact the old man and let him know the heat's on, and if you'll pardon the pun, to put this operation on ice. He may as well. It's beginning to crack at the seams." Her voice softened. "Don't look at me with such loathing. You know I'm right. I'm not clever, but you know I'm talking sense."

"You're talking sense," said Lila dully, "but as to not being clever . . . well . . . it takes more than a dummy to figure out the Rio bit. Who advised you, Hagar? Who murdered Clay Stopley?"

"Lila, when you were a little girl, you were so terribly pretty. And right now, you're so terribly ugly.' She turned and swept from the balcony into the bedroom.

Lila clenched her fists and brought them together. Her eyes were misty with tears, and she fought back a sob rising in her throat. The fists unclenched, and her hands wiped at her eyes. She reached for the bottle of beer and gently shook it. The beer foamed, and Lila whispered to the bottle, "I'm glad there's still some life in something around here."

6

"They thought I was going back to my hotel, but instead I led them here." Norton was seated across the desk from Ira Sparks, who was looking grave. Boyd Gross was at the window looking down into the street.

"I don't see any white Thunderbird," said Gross. Sparks lit a cheroot. Norton was sorry his little joke had backfired. He hadn't expected the two hoods to follow him into the police station. He had thought that when he parked he would catch a glimpse of what he was sure would be very startled expressions on their faces, but he had been denied even that. When he turned into the street where the station was located, the white Thunderbird didn't follow, as though familiar with the street and his destination. Perhaps a Judas goat might have been more successful.

Sparks finally spoke. "You're playing games with two deadly killers."

Norton responded to the melodramatic statement with: "Then why aren't they behind bars?"

"They have been," said Gross.

"They always get sprung," said Sparks. "They're hit men for the Mafia."

"You said that naughty name, I didn't." Norton crossed a leg and scratched his chest.

"It's a very fashionable name today," said Sparks. "It's big box office. You think Hagar Simon's tied in with them?"

"Or tied to somebody who's tied in with them."

"Maybe those two in the Thunderbird killed Stopley."

"Maybe."

"But you're not ready to buy it."

"I'm not looking for bargains. What're their names?"

"The blond one's Vince Hayes." They heard a chair groan as Gross settled into it. "The redhead's Tom Gucci."

Norton straightened up. "Any relation to Salvatore Gucci?"

"His grandson."

"I thought the Gucci clan went to earth after the old man got exiled back to Italy."

"Tom's a rebel," offered Gross dryly. "He came west about five years ago after his old man had half his head shot off on the front lawn of his house in Hackensack. He was Salvatore's eldest. They never did collar his killer, did they, Ira?"

"Not that I heard," replied Sparks. "Not that anybody cared," he added, "since it didn't trigger off another of their internecine gang wars."

"I know the case well," said Norton. "Just before Cristo Gucci was found dead on his front lawn, there was a rumor going around that he was thinking of making a deal with the government. The big Mafia roundup was on at the time, and Cristo was looking to save his own skin. It was said at the time that old Salvatore back in Italy got wind of it and had his own son fingered."

Sparks smiled. "That sounds like Burton Hartley. The *old* Burton Hartley."

Norton massaged an ear lobe. "Ira, I've got definite proof Clay Stopley was at Hagar Simon's Monday night."

Sparks pulled the cheroot from his mouth. "Karen Frost talked?"

Norton stared at him for a moment and then said, "I promised my informant complete protection. You'll have to go along with this."

"Sure. You're running this show." Norton could tell Ira Sparks was very unhappy. Sparks stared at the lighted end of the cheroot. "You've been covering a lot of territory." Norton had told Sparks about the people he had interviewed, then advised him he was being trailed by Vince Hayes and Tom Gucci. When he told him about the previous evening at Czardi's with Miklos, Lila Frank and Marti Leigh, he described the four dour-looking men who had occupied the adjoining table.

"More Mafia," interjected Gross. "Everybody knows Czardi's place is a front. But what the hell, if we closed down all their hangouts, there'd be no place left to eat."

"I have a suspicion Czardi was at Hagar's Monday night," said Norton.

Sparks shifted in his swivel chair. "I know what you're thinking, but believe me, the only thing Czardi kills is appetites."

"He's a nervous man, and I think a very frightened man. I wouldn't dismiss him too casually."

"My sister was married to a Hungarian dentist," said Gross. "After the divorce, he got the house, and she kept her caps."

"Oh, dry up," growled Sparks.

"Ira, what have you got on Lila Frank?"

Sparks furrowed his brows. "What do you mean, what have I 'got' on her?"

Norton screwed up his face. "Now let me think . . . she told me she's been in the big time for about three years now. Where was she before that? What was she? Who was she?"

Sparks seemed chagrined. "I should imagine she was always Lila Frank. She was out of town when Stopley was killed."

"Yes, we know where she was." Sparks and Gross exchanged looks.

"She's a very capable lady," said Gross.

"Oh, that she is," agreed Norton. "I think she's capable of decoding Stonehenge. I've got a date with her tonight. She's taking me to a party at Hagar Simon's."

"Fast work," said Sparks.

"Faster than I hoped. Too fast," he added cryptically, without elaborating on his personal suspicion that the evening was a hastily put together setup to throw him off the scent, "but I'd like to think Hagar's appetite has been whetted for a taste of me."

"I have to hand it to you, Norton. You draw yourself a straight line and then you follow it."

"Anybody who thinks I'm following a straight line is a square." He embellished the statement with his stupid grin by way of assuring Sparks no offense was intended. "It's how I've always worked, Ira. I charge into every assignment like a bull in a china shop."

"Fox in a chicken coop's more like it," said Gross wryly.

"Anything to stir up a commotion, Boyd. Panic causes confusion, and confusion leads to errors, and I'm beginning to profit." He thought about mentioning Viola Fairbanks's slip about the madras jacket but as quickly realized it could lead to Chloe Jupiter as his informant. He guided them back to Lila Frank. "Lila moves in very strange and very mysterious ways. She was presumably in New York for five days on business, but we happen to know she squeezed in a quick hop to Europe."

Sparks tightened his briefly slack jaw. "Maybe she went there to get laid."

"She's made a great many clandestine trips to Europe over the past three years."

"Collecting news is part of her job, isn't it?" said Sparks.

"Whatever compels her, she's been making an unusual amount of trips abroad. She covers her tracks well. We don't know where she goes."

Boyd suggested, "Maybe you should tie a bell around her neck."

Sparks pushed his chair back and stood up. "You know, Norton, I don't think it's so healthy the way you're playing footsie with us. Now, just you listen for a change, and hear me out. You Feds don't ask for cooperation; you command it. You can understand some of us get a little tired of this tug of war between the federal and the municipal governments. You've got something on Hagar, and it's big. How big we have to judge for ourselves. You're not just out to break up orgies and arrest pot smokers. That's small pickings today. You boys are out to make a grand slam. You hold all the cards, and you're shuffling them and dealing them the way you see fit. Well, you ain't been doing so hot, have you? You've lost one man, and, for all I know, there were others before him."

"There weren't." Norton was lighting a cigarette, looking as suave as an old-time matinee idol.

Sparks leaned on the desk sternly. "Thanks for *that*. Stopley gets himself bumped off and deposited in Griffith Park like a sack of garbage." Norton broke the dead match in two pieces and dropped them slowly into an ashtray. "Well, when a stiff is found within my jurisdiction, it's my job to find his killer. We're cooperating with you boys, but not at the expense of being made to look like a bunch of pricks. I should be out breaking down every one of those lying alibis, but you're tying my hands." He wagged a beefy index finger under Norton's nose. "I could get a writ issued and be inside Hagar's place in an hour."

"To look for what? Cover the ramparts to look for traces of blood? You won't find a damn thing. You're three days too late." Norton's voice hardened. "And Clay Stopley wasn't any mothering sack of garbage. He was a good operator who got tripped up, the way lots of good anybody's get tripped up. I could get tripped up. You and Boyd could stop a bullet because you were too slow to duck. It's as important to us to find Clay's murderer as it is to you. You want to go out and third-degree Hagar's guests . . . friends . . . associates— however the hell you choose to label them—you go right ahead. You want to pull in Tom Gucci and Vince Hayes with charges of suspicion of harassing a private citizen, you do that too. They'll be replaced this fast . . ." he snapped his fingers, and Gross winced, ". . . by another pair of jokers. You said it yourself, Ira. I've accomplished a hell of a lot in a short space of time. I don't know if I'm that smart or that lucky or just another sitting duck. You think I'm not wondering and examining why it is moving all this fast for me? Don't you think I'm suspicious I might be following a trail of carefully laid red herrings? Don't you think I get the cold sweats at the prospect of ending up in Griffith Park as another . . ." he spat each word venomously, ". . . sack of garbage?" He simmered down quickly and reacted with a smile at the puckish expression on Boyd Gross's face. "What's so funny?"

"Your fly's open."

Norton looked down and pulled up his zipper. "I'll have to find me a new tailor." Sparks was at the window with his back to the others, his hands clenched together behind him. It reminded Norton of his father, wondering what punishment to mete out for a youthful peccadillo. He looked at Boyd Gross and shrugged. Gross winked back. Norton felt that in this placid man he might have a friend and an ally. He wished the positions were reversed, with Gross in charge of the investigation of Clay Stopley's murder. It wasn't a matter of distrusting Ira Sparks; it was just that he instinctively knew with Boyd Gross there could be his kind of communication, the kind enjoyed with his superior back in Washington, the kind he used to share with Clay Stopley, regardless of Clay's brief fall from grace after his one-night stand with Marti. Norton shoved his hands in his trouser pockets and began pacing the room slowly. He was searching for the right approach to Ira Sparks. He understood what the man was up against, the feelings of impotence and inadequacy and frustration, possibly even jealousy, emotions that had frequently plagued Norton when caught in a similar situation.

"I know what's rubbing you the wrong way, Ira." Sparks moved his head slightly and saw Norton from the corner of an eye. "But for the time being, I have to ask you to go along with me. I can't tell you yet where I got my information nailing Clay's presence at Hagar's Monday night. One corpse in this case is already one corpse too many. We don't want another one, do we?"

Sparks replied, as he moved back to his desk, "Nobody likes a crowded morgue. But how do you know this bunch won't start killing each other? They're going to know somebody's grassed, because you're going to let them know."

"That's right."

"So they start doing some detective work of their own. Maybe they smart-guess, maybe they don't. They start distrusting each other . . ."

"You're getting on my wavelength, Ira. That's just what I'm hoping for. Divide and conquer. We can safely guess that, as far as they're concerned, Clay's killing was a deplorable error. So I don't think he died because he got the goods we're after. I think he stumbled on something or someone at Hagar's that caused brute panic. Somebody he knew. Somebody he recognized." *Marti?* Norton cleared his throat. "Maybe somebody from the past whose presence there opened a fresh can of peas for him. He was probably already drugged by this time, but probably not drugged enough. Clay might have wandered away from the main body of the party and found someone he shouldn't have found there. This person panicked and used violence. I can't reconstruct for you what might have happened, because I'm not clairvoyant. But I'll tell you this, the people who pay Hagar would have found a more sophisticated means of getting rid of Clay. They wouldn't have dumped him in Griffith Park. We wouldn't have found his body this soon, if at all. He would have vanished into thin air, making the job that much tougher for us.

"So whoever blundered did us a favor and Hagar's gang a disservice. I have grave doubts as to whether anybody at that party witnessed Clay's killing."

"Why?" asked Sparks huskily.

"Because we'd have had a second corpse. Either the witness . . . or Clay's killer. All that those frightened guests know is Clay was there and died on the premises. So they've been threatened into this conspiracy of silence. Now there's just one person who might know or suspect what happened to Clay, and that's Karen Frost. I said 'might,' Ira. It's a toss-up why she got that black eye and who delivered the punch. One thing's for sure, she didn't fall off any horse, unless she's got one on rockers in her bedroom."

"We should take her into protective custody," insisted Sparks.

"I'd rather you put a tail on her. Let's find out who visits her or who she's visiting. I don't think she'll be moving out of that apartment very much with that mouse on her eye."

Sparks nodded. "What about Lila Frank . . . Czardi . . . the rest of them . . ."

"I'm just trying to start a little war of nerves. Easiest way to get a structure to shake is to start picking away at the foundations. You'd be surprised how one frightened person can start an epidemic of fear. And frightened people start making all the wrong moves. Czardi, for instance, may not be all that important in this scheme of things, but I've started him sweating. Karen Frost feeds me a bum alibi and then tries to shore it up with an equally feeble assist from this Marti Leigh." He spoke her name hoarsely and covered it by drawing a drink of water from the cooler in the room. "Viola Fairbanks is a dumb little bunny terrified of her aunt. Viola's too dimwitted to know or understand what's going on around her. A paper towel absorbs more. But you don't pigeonhole your dimwits either. Sometimes they make important slips without knowing they've made them." Like madras jacket. "Chloe Jupiter's a tough old bird. She's got one thing going for her the others seem to sadly lack, a great sense of humor. That's what makes her a survivor, and Chloe intends to outlive all of us. So I don't get all that much out of her."

He knew Sparks was swallowing, but how much was he digesting? Had Norton's ears wiggled or his nose twitched

— 89 —

while discussing Chloe? He could sense from the expression on the detective's face he was doing his damnedest to figure out the identity of Norton's informant.

"And then we have Lila Frank. Knows all; sees all; hears all; tells nothing, except what she hopes will please her readers and viewers. A spectacular rise to power in the short span of three years. Who helped it happen that swiftly? Why all the mysterious trips to Europe? If they're innocent, why go to such extravagant lengths to cover her tracks? She's got our entire European operation buffaloed." He smiled. "But I've got her worried. Talk about drawing straight lines, Sparks, she's leading me directly to Hagar. She's saving me precious time. Now, why is that brassy lady being such a darling?"

"Maybe she's after your body," suggested Sparks.

"Dead or alive?"

"Oh, alive, I should think," said Sparks as he shifted in his chair. "I doubt if the lady's a necrophiliac."

"Let's hope not. Ira, Hagar's an old friend of yours."

"Ahhh, Norton, I haven't seen her in years. Not since she stopped doing those personal appearances."

"But you said she was a good Joe in those days."

"One of the sweetest."

"Pushed into marriage by her mother with a man at least thirty years her senior."

"But Isaac was good to her."

"Sure, he was good to her. He destroyed himself being good to her. Now, somebody else is being good to her. For private reasons, Hagar's been put back on top of the world. A pretty shaky world, but she's right back up there. Somebody smarter than Isaac, more powerful." He thought for a moment. "Hagar Holt. What is she originally? Dutch? Swedish?"

It was Boyd Gross who answered him. "Swiss. She competed in the Olympics when she was a kid. Some promoter brought her here for one of them touring ice shows, and when they played L.A., Isaac saw her. That right, Ira?"

Sparks nodded and set a match to a fresh cheroot.

Norton continued. "So little Hagar travels with her mother, obviously a very domineering lady."

"Very," said Sparks after blowing a smoke ring.

"And Hagar gets pushed into a loveless marriage. No back talk. No sass. Just says, 'Okay, Mama, if you want me to marry him, I'll marry him.' But Hagar's a healthy young filly. Where does she get her kicks? Wouldn't you think she might have had some lovers on the side?"

Sparks flicked an ash. "Doesn't everybody?"

"No gossip about her?"

"None I ever heard," said Sparks. "You ever hear of her having any hanky panky, Boyd?"

"Nah, I don't read gossip columns." He smiled at Norton. "That sounds like one for Lila Frank."

"I'm making a mental note." Norton realized he was still holding the empty paper cup, crumpled it, and tossed it into the wastepaper basket. "Well, I better be getting back to the hotel. I've got some phone calls to make. Have we made peace, Ira?"

"Oh, sure," Sparks said lavishly, "you know how it is. Guy's got to let off steam every so often. This isn't the greatest job in the world, you know."

"I know. I don't envy you. And there's them that don't envy me. That's what makes a horse race. I wish I was coming down the stretch."

"Maybe you are, and you don't know it," suggested Gross.

"I'll know it when it's happening. Little bells go off in my head, and they're not the little bells you hear on an ice cream wagon." Gross was out of his chair and following Norton to the door.

"I'm going to grab some lunch, Ira. Be back in half an hour." Sparks grunted. Gross opened the door for Norton. Norton looked at Sparks behind the desk, now busying himself with papers. He thought of saying something by way of farewell, but nothing came to mind, except, "I'll be in touch." Sparks responded with another grunt, and Norton and Gross left.

Hearing the door shut, Sparks looked up. His fist closed

over a sheaf of papers, crumpling them in one ferocious movement. He kicked his chair back, jumped to his feet, and hurled the crumpled mass at the door.

"Son of a bitch. Snot-nosed son of a bitch."

Norton wasn't surprised by Boyd Gross's invitation to join him for a sandwich or coffee. He could tell back in the office there was something on the detective's mind and had been hoping it was something he wanted to share with Norton. They were settled in the booth of a sparsely filled luncheonette around the corner from police headquarters. The counterman and waitress knew Gross, and there had been a quick exchange of jocular inanities. Norton could see Gross was an easily liked man. He was younger than Ira Sparks, probably in his late thirties, Norton guessed, and the thin gold band on the third finger of his left hand answered another vital statistic. Norton hoped the marriage was a happy one.

"Norton," began Gross, while building a pyramid with sugar cubes, "I once took a course in applied psychology. I went to night school. It was my wife's suggestion. She got tired of hearing me beef about Ira Sparks."

"Now you've learned to love him."

"I don't love him. But now I can live with him. You see, poor old Ira's that crappy cliché, a cop's cop. He's damned good at his job. It's all he's got. He's a lonely man, a bitter man, and—I know I can trust you wih this one—he's a diabetic. I don't know too much about his background because Ira's a very private man. I know he's a bachelor, lives in a three-room walkup in West L.A., doesn't seem to have many friends, if any, and if he's got a girl friend, it's the best kept secret in town. What I know for sure is that he dreams of retirement. The bottom drawer of his desk is filled with travel brochures. He's been with the force for over twenty years, and he's never won a medal or a citation."

"An unsung hero."

"He just prefers anonymity. He's also a very jealous man, and you're making him very jealous."

"Ira could use that course in applied psychology."

Gross smiled. "He's jealous of the way you operate. He thinks you're glamorous."

"When next we meet, should I kiss him?"

The waitress arrived on that line and gave Norton a peculiar look. Gross saw the look and chuckled. They ordered chicken sandwiches and coffee, and the waitress departed for the kitchen, after another quick look over her shoulder at Norton. "I think you've just given Sadie the wrong impression."

Norton lifted a sugar cube from Gross's pyramid and tossed it from hand to hand. "You boys should know by now how the secret service works. We're trained to share just so much information and no more. We're also trained to respect the people we work with. I don't know if I like or dislike Ira Sparks, and it really doesn't matter, as long as I'm getting the cooperation I need." He paused to think before making his next statement and then decided to go ahead with it. "Clay Stopley didn't like Ira."

"Didn't like or didn't trust?"

Norton dropped the sugar cube back in the bowl. "You're a smart lad, Gross." He folded his hands on the table and leaned forward. "We've had trouble with the police before. You know law enforcement bureaus resent each other's guts. Everybody's looking for a laurel wreath, even if it's a lousy fit."

"And every time you meet a cop, you're wondering if this is the one that's corrupted."

"That's right. In the sort of organization we suspect Hagar is involved with, corruption is an old and trusted friend. It's like the Dark Ages again, Boyd. There's a new breed of Borgias and Machiavellis. How do I know Hagar's people don't have a pipeline to yours?"

Gross began dismantling his pyramid. "I guess you think it's a gamble breaking bread with me."

"I think it's a gamble every time I use a bathroom."

Sadie was back with the sandwiches and coffee. She had a look of distaste, as though facing the prospect of sharing a park bench with a tramp. Norton was amazed she didn't slosh the coffee. He watched her return to the counter, while Gross busied himself with his food. After swallowing the first bite, Gross said, "If anybody's on the take around our place, we haven't had a hint of it. But that doesn't mean it might not be happening. I've been tempted in my time. I guess most of us have."

"Are you applying psychology?" Norton was applying mustard.

"No, just leveling. I'm disgustingly honest and true-blue because I married a chubby conscience who uses too much henna." Norton laughed. "Her name's Bessie, and every time she reads about some schmuck cop getting busted, she waves the newspaper in my face and yells, 'Sweetheart, this had better never be you.' Ah, hell," he reached for a paper napkin and wiped his fingers vigorously, "this isn't what our little chat was supposed to be about. I feel sorry for Ira, that's all. That's all I'm trying to tell you. He doesn't know how to deal with you. He didn't know how to deal with Stopley. He kept calling him Rover Boy. Maybe I should have gone with him to the hotel when he met him."

"Clay didn't come to the station?"

"No. He asked Ira to the hotel. The first time I met Stopley was in Griffith Park. Ira never stopped grousing after he got back from that meeting. And, like he told you, he didn't like Stopley not keeping in touch. At least, you're handling that side better."

"Well, this time we've got a murder. It overlaps my basic assignment. If I can kill two birds, all the better. I've only kept one fact from you boys, and that's because for the time being it suits my purpose. And my purpose is what's important."

"Agreed. I think Ira understands that too. It's just that he's never learned how to be a subordinate. He doesn't like taking a backseat. That's why he worked so hard to get off the beat."

"I know you're on my side, Boyd. Put in a good word for me. If I get to Clay's killer first, I promise I'll turn him over to you boys. But I hope the murdering has stopped with Clay."

Boyd's hand holding the coffee cup froze in midair. "You think there might be *more?*"

"I'm always prepared for any eventualities. I was on the team investigating John Kennedy's assassination. There was a chain reaction of very sudden, very mysterious deaths. Some we found out why; some we're still wondering about. It taught me to be prepared. You know that old saw about the Mafia. They only kill each other. Want me to draw pictures where this case is concerned?" He reached into his pocket and withdrew his billfold.

"This tab's mine," protested Boyd. "I invited you."

"I've got a bigger expense account." Norton dropped a bill on the table with an expansive gesture that didn't escape Sadie at the counter. She hastily totaled the tab on her pad and crossed the room with it.

"Will there be anything else?" Sadie's voice betrayed enlarged adenoids.

Norton said with a smile, "Only a worshipful glance." Sadie grabbed the bill from the table and hurried away. Norton broke into Boyd's preoccupation. "Putting a tail on Karen Frost is a very good idea. I hope Ira's following through."

"He's taken care of it by now. Ira may not look it, but he's very thorough. About Lila Frank, I'll start backtracking her. I know you're planning to put your own tracers on her."

"So what? Every little bit helps. I could also use anything you've got on Burton Hartley."

"Off the top of my head, I can tell you he's a lush . . ."

"Fairly common knowledge."

"We've pulled him in on a variety of drunk driving charges, all quashed by someone up there . . ."

"Understandable."

"And for the past couple of years, he's been writing as though somebody's castrated his typewriter."

"He still manages to scoop a couple of juicy plums every

now and then. But he was at Hagar's Monday night. And I hope he's going to be there tonight. I'm even toying with a crack at Udo Yosaka."

"You'll have to do that by long distance."

"He's skipped?"

"Sorry. Should have told you earlier. He flew back to Hawaii last night." Norton's fingers drummed a tattoo on the table, as Sadie returned with his change. "We had no reason to try and hold him." Norton handed Sadie a dollar bill and, from the change of expression on her face, wondered if she had decided to fall in love with him.

"Well, gee . . . thanks a lot," said Sadie, and she hurried away.

Norton was dwelling on the departed Japanese business-man. "I guess you're right, Boyd. If it's necessary, our bureau in Hawaii can get to him." They struggled out of their cramped quarters. Norton clapped a friendly hand on Boyd's shoulder. "Your heart's in the right place, Boyd."

"Well, they pay me to keep the peace." He waved goodbye to Sadie and the counterman and accompanied Norton to the Renault. Norton got behind the wheel and gunned the engine, while Gross's eyes scanned the area for any sign of the white Thunderbird. "I think your friends may have knocked off for lunch."

"Any bets?" Norton put the car in to gear and shouted, "Have a nice day!"

Gross grinned and gave a salutatory wave as the Renault pulled away. He watched Norton make a right turn toward Hollywood and then entered the station house.

Norton whistled under his breath, while thinking about his conversation with Boyd Gross. A lot had been said. Some-thing had been left unsaid. Norton was wise enough to realize Gross hadn't been jockeying for position in his favor at the expense of Ira Sparks. Gross was the kind of man who would make it on his own and on his own terms, or he'd have to answer to that chubby, henna-haired conscience. Or was Norton trying to read too much into the purpose of the impromptu luncheon invitation? He had to admit to himself, Sparks fascinated him. He was the kind of man who rarely entered Norton's social orbit. He was coarse-hewn and tough, a man whose record carried admirable recommendations. The bureau had checked him out thoroughly. Professional life unblemished. Private life likewise. Private life such as it is.

Hello there! The white Thunderbird was back in his rearview mirror. Now that he knew the names of the two villains, Norton almost felt friendlier toward them. It was still redheaded Tom Gucci at the wheel, and Norton wondered if they ever spelled each other. Were their girlfriends annoyed because they were devoting so much time to Norton? Did they go to church? Were they good to their mothers? Norton almost passed a red light and bore down on the brakes. He heard the screech of brakes behind him and turned around. Vince Hayes had hit his head against the windshield, and it didn't need a lipreader to figure out the imprecations he was mouthing. Gucci was responding with a series of obscene Sicilian gestures. Norton thought the act was almost funny enough to be booked into Las Vegas.

Twenty minutes later, the Renault was parked in the garage under the hotel, and Norton was lying on the couch in his living room talking into the turquoise phone. The monotonous voice coming from the receiver was telling him that Count Miklos Czardi was a bogus nobleman. He had entered the country illegally some thirty years ago. He had led the immigration authorities a merry chase for over two decades before settling in Hollywood and opening his restaurant. Legal action was instigated against him and then quickly and mysteriously dropped. The file on him remained open, however, and if Norton thought it would help to revive the prosecution . . .

"Not yet," interjected Norton sharply. "It may come in handy, but let's keep it in the deep freeze a while longer. Any line on who's been protecting him?" Norton was told the name of an Eastern congressman. It was a familiar name. It was a name listed in the dossier on Hagar Simon. Norton changed the subject to Udo Yosaka. He repeated what little information he had on the man's presence at the castle on Monday night. He repeated carefully his interviews with Viola Fairbanks and Chloe Jupiter, followed by his session in Ira Sparks's office and his luncheon with Boyd Gross. He cited the names of the two men tailing him. He spoke carefully and enunciated clearly because he knew he was being tape-recorded at the other end. Then he requested as thorough an investigation as possible into the origins of Lila Frank. He followed this with the advice that he would be escorting her to Hagar Simon's that night. He heard an obscene suggestion from the other end of the wire and replied that he would take it under consideration, but would only act on it if it was strictly in the line of duty. For want of a better sign-off, he blew kisses into the mouthpiece and then hung up.

He arose from the couch and began removing his sweaty shirt. He stifled a yawn as he crossed to the window and looked out at the pool. He was thinking of paying another call on Karen Frost, when he noticed the fat bimbo Ira Sparks had admired the previous afternoon. She was stretched out on a chaise unabashedly wearing a bikini, looking like a blob of dough that contained too much yeast. She was deep in conversation with a very gorgeous creature wearing a one-piece bathing suit, the style of which told him it had been manufactured abroad. The owner of the bathing suit was gently applying suntan lotion to her long, shapely legs. She wore sunglasses, and her luxurious mane of hair was tied behind her head with a pink ribbon.

Norton felt the stirring in his loins, the stirring he would always feel at the sight of Marti Leigh.

7

"It looked like a very dull day, until I saw you sitting out here."

Norton had changed into violet and yellow swim trunks and had a bath towel casually slung over his right shoulder. He was easing himself into the chaise next to Marti. The fat redhead raised her head for an appraising look at Norton, while Marti made a good show of looking perplexed and wondering who he was.

"Norton Valentine," he said, sounding slighted that anyone could ever forget him. "Last night at Czardi's?"

"Oh, for heaven's sake, of course!" exclaimed Marti in a delectable assortment of vocal tones, "I didn't recognize you without your clothes on." She turned to the fat redhead. "Ella May, this is Norton Valentine." Her neck swiveled back to Norton. "This is my friend, Ella May Rudge."

"Nice to meet you, Ella May."

Ella May's cavern of a mouth opened and shut rapidly like a dolphin contemplating a herring, and then she lazily waved her right hand. "Howary'all, Nawton." There was Blue Ridge Mountains in her voice and pagan lust in her face, and Norton felt like a Christmas turkey.

"Staying here at the Dauphin?" Norton asked Marti.

"No, just visiting with Ella May."

"Y'all restin' heah, Nawton?" Ella May had heaved herself into a sitting position and removed her sunglasses. Norton pointed to his apartment. "H'come we ain't seen y'all heah at the pool befo'?"

"I didn't want to break any hearts."

Ella May erupted with a bellowing laugh, and Norton momentarily expected the appearance of a herdsman. "Y'hear that, Marti honey?" Ella May thwacked Marti's thigh, and Marti looked as though she needed a bullet to bite on. "He didn' wanna break any hearts! Well, now, ain't he somethin'?" She licked her lips and winked at Norton. He wished he was wearing armor.

"Ella May's in town for a recording session," Marti told Norton, who wondered if she meant a seismograph. "She's a big name in country and western records." Norton was thinking Ella May belonged on a platter with an apple in her mouth. "She usually records in Nashville, but she has a new contract with Trump Records. Their studios are here in L.A."

"Yeah, it's the real big time fer li'l ol' me now. Sure do miss the folks back home, tho'. Got a call inter them right now. Ah'm sure gonna slobber into that phone when I git it." Norton had no reason to doubt her. "It's mighty lonely heah fer a li'l ol' country gal like me. Cain't find nobody to take me dancin'. Ah bet yer pretty quick on yer feet, Nawton, ain'tcha?"

Norton thought fast. "I used to be before I tore my Achilles tendon playing tennis. My dancing days are over now."

Ella May clucked her tongue. "Po' li'l thing. If'n yer like, ah'll come over an' massage that leg o' yours later, huh?"

Norton blanched. "Er . . . uh . . . well, we'll see . . . I . . ."

The poolside loudspeaker interrupted, paging Ella May. "Thank God," Norton said under his breath.

"Ella May's comin', honey!" she shouted as she heaved

herself off the chaise. They watched her lumber toward the lobby eagerly, as though answering the mating call of a bull elephant.

"Ella May's such a darling," said Marti mellifluously. "She hasn't been feeling too well since she got here."

"Anthrax?"

"Lay off. She's a nice kid. I met her in London last year when she was doing some p.a.'s. She's got a glorious voice, but unfortunately she's not terribly bright. She still thinks the earth is flat."

"You've certainly been getting around since our late unpleasantness. Hong-King . . . London . . . Hagar Simon's."

"That's me . . . nymph errant. Cigarette?" She reached under her chaise, and a duffel bag materialized. They lit cigarettes and settled back. They sat in silence for a few moments, Norton with so much to ask, not knowing where to begin. Finally he spoke.

"Thanks for not giving the game away last night."

"Save it. They have their suspicions about you."

"I mean about our having been married."

"That was for my own protection. I had to play the game with Clay last Monday night."

"You're slipping. I'm not supposed to know he was there. You were supposed to be in Palm Springs."

Marti flicked an ash and turned to him. "They know you know he was there, and I know you know Palm Springs was a clumsy alibi. Karen never told me which eye got smacked."

They know you know he was there. But how? If Chloe had decided to tell someone she had spilled the beans, why? She'd been adamant that morning about being protected. It couldn't have been Chloe. It had to be something else. Maybe Chloe's house was bugged after all. He'd think about that later. Here was Marti to be dealt with.

"Who smacked Karen in the eye?"

"She hasn't said, but she's plenty frightened."

"Why hasn't she said?" he persisted.

"In her own words, Nortie . . . 'Marti, it's better you don't know.'"

"Did she see Clay get it?"

She raised her legs until the knees almost touched her chin as she leaned forward and hugged them. "I don't know. I really don't know. But she obviously saw something. She didn't want to see you last night. She didn't want to see you ever, but somebody told her to."

"So she saw me, and she was badly rehearsed."

"Norton." He turned to her, and her eyes were electric. "Karen was in love with Clay, very deeply in love with him. Girls like Karen don't fall in love like that."

Or girls like Marti.

"You're not listening to me."

"I hear every word, Marti. What do you know about what's going on at Hagar's?"

"I don't know anything," she said with irritation. "Czardi's her friend, and I'm his friend, and that's how I met her."

"I'd have thought you could do better than that Hungarian greaseball."

Her voice became unattractive. "He's just a *friend*. There's nothing else. If anybody's, he's Lila Frank's."

"You've got to be joking."

She took a nervous puff on the cigarette. "She told me, when he gets out of the bathtub, he leaves an oil slick."

"That certainly sounds like Lila. What do you know about her?"

Marti opened her palm expressively. "As much as you or anybody else knows. You mean her family? Where she comes from? I haven't the slightest. It's never occurred to me to ask."

"Okay. What did they feed Clay Monday night?"

"I don't know what it was, but you're right. He was on something. It couldn't have been very much, because he never made a slip about the two of us having known each other before. I was a nervous wreck the whole damned evening."

"Why? What were you afraid of?"

"Oh, stop playing the ass. Don't you think I figured he was at Hagar's on an assignment? Monday wasn't the first time I'd met him there. He'd been there before with Karen and . . ." She caught herself too late.

"So you saw Clay twice. Shall we try for three? Lunch? Cocktails? Did you just happen to be here at the pool one afternoon, and you ran into each other? Come on, Marti. Loosen up those tight lips. Did the two of you toss off a quick one for old time's sake?"

"You *shit*." Her cigarette was almost burnt down to her fingers, and she flung it to the ground with a vehemence, then looked at him with eyes blazing. "I wish I could lie about it just to make you suffer." Anger mercurially gave way to amusement. "Good heavens, Nortie, you're still jealous. Am I having it off with Czardi? Was there another quickie with Clay? Why, Nortie, darling, I'm absolutely flattered. This is your first time at the pool, so that slight tan of yours must have come from the torch you're carrying."

Norton said through clenched teeth, "I'm glad I've made you happy at last." He leaned over and ground out his cigarette butt on the ground without taking his eyes from Marti.

"Don't horse around with me, baby. You're playing with the grown-ups now. You're not posing for Avedon with six layers of gauze over the lens. You're into a lethal situation here, and you'd better start reassessing your priorities. Clay's been murdered. That's no catbird seat your friend Karen's sitting on. You saw Clay a third time, and he trusted you enough to flesh out some of the details of his assignment." *And if he did, and you betrayed him, as much as I still love you, I'll kill you.*

"I saw him at Karen's late Sunday afternoon. She invited me over for a drink. I didn't know he was going to be there.

That's the truth, Norton." She was waiting to see the skepticism erased from his eyes but she wasn't rewarded. "I felt awkward and stupid, but he carried it off brilliantly. He was his smooth, funny, silly old self. He made the same old idiotic puns and went through the great performance of mixing the perfect dry vodka martini . . ." her voice softened, ". . . while Karen devoured him with her eyes, and I envied the way she felt. Oh, hell, Nortie, I was seeing myself when we first met."

"Christ, Marti. What the hell have you gotten yourself into? What have you been living on? Who's footing the bills? Are you involved with some Mafia big shot you met abroad?"

"Go soak your head." The ground beneath Norton's chaise began to tremble. He saw Ella May Rudge returning, looking like the leading balloon in the Macy's Thanksgiving Day Parade. "My, my! Y'all both look like y'just seen a plane crash."

Marti forced a smile. "How was the family?"

"Right chipper. Ah'm goin' right inside 'n' pencil them a letter." She was gathering up her belongings with a nimbleness that belied her size. "Now, Marti, y'all cum tap on m' door befo' y'go now, y'heah?"

"I'll be along in a few minutes."

"An', Nawton, ah'm in room two-oh-nine, should y'change y'mind about that theah massage. Y'real cute, Nawton. See y'soon!" She stomped away from them, while Marti averted her eyes from Norton.

"What's your connection with Hagar?"

"We're acquaintances. And that's all."

"You're lying." Marti made a move to leave, and Norton grabbed her wrist. "This isn't fun and games, and we aren't having a lark. This is a deadly business you're mixed up in."

Marti slapped his hand away, fully aware most eyes at the poolside were upon her and Norton. "Cool it, Nortie. We're the star attraction. We're only supposed to have met last night, remember?" She spoke rapidly and under her breath. "You don't know who the rest of these jokers are, do you?

You want this scene reported to Lila or Hagar or whoever the hell? You think I'd go out of my way to spend time with that sorry tub of lard?" She suddenly laughed graciously, produced her pack of cigarettes, and gaily offered him one. "Smile, dear, we're on 'Candid Camera,' and be a gentleman and light these cigarettes." He took her Zippo and ignited it. Cigarettes aglow, she retrieved the lighter, dropped it in the bag, and set it to one side. "Now then, I'll tell you exactly what I told Clay when I saw him for the *fourth* time." Norton lay back staring at the sky and waited. "We had lunch Monday afternoon. He made a point of inviting both Karen and myself, knowing Karen had a modeling assignment and couldn't make it. And I told him this. I met Czardi at a dinner party in Hong-Kong." She mentioned the name of a Chinese film producer. It sounded like something Norton might have selected from Column A. "I wanted to get back to the States. I was short of cash, and I could see he was interested. Just don't say anything. Just lie there and listen. Yes, I'd been mixed up with somebody, and I wanted out. I told that to Czardi, and my timing was right. I was just what the doctor ordered. He offered me a plane ticket and a bonus to carry a package back here and get it through customs. Presumably it was perfume. Don't say it . . ." He had started to speak, and she was in no mood to be interrupted. "I could figure it out for myself. Heroin, hash . . . whatever. I was desperate enough to gamble and accept the offer.

"Once safely through customs, he paid me off and tried a pass. I politely let him know it was no soap, and he didn't push it. But he did say he knew how I could pick up some more of the green stuff, if I was interested. I was interested. I needed a new wardrobe and a long stay at Main Chance to get back into shape before going to New York to see if I can pick up my modeling career again. He told me about Hagar and how much she pays her girls." She heard his quick intake of breath and said softly, "I promise you, Nortie, I haven't sunk to professional prostitution. I'm just paid to be decoration, be nice to the more important guests from out of town, get them drunk, share the weed, get them talking . . . anything, everything . . ."

"Everything on tape . . . whenever possible on film . . ."

"Norton, I thought it was a private enterprise at first. You have to believe that. It wasn't until I saw Clay . . . it wasn't until then . . . Norton?" When speaking his name, she sounded like a sad little girl, and he turned to her. "He told me what I was really mixed up in. And when I read he'd been murdered . . . I . . . oh, hell . . ." She turned her face away.

"Let's go back to Monday night. When was the last time you saw Clay?"

She took a drag of her cigarette and thought for a moment. "I remember he was with Karen and Hagar. We could see he was high on something, and Karen was upset. I was with Czardi and Burton Hartley, who was high as a kite and giving us trouble. I saw Hagar leave Karen and Clay and go out. Karen was pleading with Clay, and then that Jap . . . can't remember his name . . ."

"Udo Yosaka."

"He came up to Karen and engaged her in conversation. When Karen's back was turned that Clay slipped away, presumably in search of Hagar. The little Jap was obviously propositioning Karen, and I could see she wanted out. I told Czardi I was going to the bathroom and left him to cope with Hartley. Nasty little drunk, Hartley. Anyway, I went over to Karen and made some excuse that Hagar was looking for her, and she lammed out after Clay. So Yosaka makes a pass at me, and I explain I'm Mr. Czardi's date. The little Pickfair thing . . . Viola . . . comes walking by, and I grab her and throw her to Yosaka. I went back to Czardi and asked him to take me home. He tried to give me an argument, but I wanted out. It took some convincing, but he finally took me home. That was the last I saw of Clay or Karen that night, and so help me, God, that is the truth."

"Who told you to lie about Clay's presence there?"

"Czardi," she said flatly.

"When was this?"

"Early the next morning. He phoned. I was still asleep."

"Didn't you ask any questions?"

"Of course, I did!"

"Didn't it occur to you then that Clay might have been dead?"

"I don't know. Maybe it did. I didn't want to think about it. I phoned Karen. She was hysterical. I got dressed and went over to her place."

"Did she have the black eye then?"

Her voice was barely audible. "Yes."

"And she wouldn't say who gave it to her?"

"No."

Something was nagging at Norton's brain. It had to do with Karen Frost, but it wouldn't crystallize. "Have you ever come across two hoods named Tom Gucci and Vince Hayes?" Norton described them.

"No. They don't ring a bell. What about them?"

"They've been on my tail since I got here. They travel in a white Thunderbird. I'm wondering if they provided a similar service for Clay."

"He never mentioned it, if he suspected he was being followed. If he was, then I could be in trouble." Norton was staring at a tub of flowers where three bees were gang-banging a daisy. "Well, *say* something."

"What do you want me to say? Sure, you're in trouble. Whether you and Clay were tailed out to the beach or not, you're in trouble. For starters, you're on Hagar's payroll."

"I can get out of that." There was a crooked smile on her face. "I've disappeared before."

"It won't be that easy this time. You're on file at the bureau now. You know how we operate. Every report I phone in is taped and transcribed. Everything I've accomplished since yesterday, everyone I've met is on the record. Did you expect me not to tell them I've run into my ex-wife? That you knew Clay? That my former beloved is now mixed up in some way with Hagar Simon, and it could give me a headache no aspirin can cure?"

She was stubbing out her cigarette on the ground. "And

that I might have ratted on both of you." He nodded. "I *told* you I haven't." He said nothing. She searched his impassive face for some sign of confidence. "Sure, Nortie. I get the picture. Guilty until proven innocent. Well, I'm willing to gamble when you get to the bottom of all this, you'll find I was on the square with you. I was a lousy wife, Nortie, but there'll always be a soft spot in my heart for you." She was gathering up her things. "It was quite a shock seeing you last night."

"Likewise."

"I know. You looked the same way on our wedding day. When I read about Clay's death, I guess somewhere in the back of my mind I knew you might be next up at bat."

"You read about Clay's death."

"You heard me," she snapped. "I *read* about it."

"When you saw Karen Tuesday morning, she didn't know he'd been murdered?"

Marti had been standing making an elaborate business of pulling the drawstrings on her duffel bag. She sat down abruptly with the bag on her lap. "Sure, she knew something had happened to him, but she never mentioned murder."

"You also knew then it was her right eye that got smacked."

"I was wondering how long it would take you to figure that one out."

Norton drew his legs up and rubbed the back of his neck. So she had gone out of her way to deliberately tip him the previous evening at Czardi's. She had snapped at his bait and not corrected him about which of Karen's eyes sported the brutal bruise. "What happens if Czardi and Lila suddenly remember you agreed it was her left eye that got hit and not her right?"

"I'll plead nerves."

He shook his head back and forth slowly. "Will wonders never cease."

"Perhaps if it had been anybody else but Clay, I might have worked harder at preserving my own skin. But not

Clay." Her voice grew faint. "And not you."

"I guess I'll never figure you out, will I?"

"If I can't, how the hell can you?" Their eyes met, and they both smiled. "I'm a fallen angel, Nortie, a woman no better than she should be, but I still have a few principles. I deliberately set out to have that fling with Clay. I was jealous, and it was childish. You and I were apart so often, I was afraid we'd forget each other's names. I guess I was never meant to be anybody's wife. Anybody's girl, but never anybody's wife."

"I still love you, Marti."

"I guess I know that, Nortie, which makes you a bigger fool than I am. You've got more important things to think about now. There's Hagar, and there's Clay. Don't get sidetracked. It might put you off your guard. I think that's what happened to Clay. I think he was in love with Karen. I think he was spending too much thought on how to protect her. Don't you waste that energy on me." She added airily. "Just try to put in a good word for me, if I ever need it. Now I better go up and go through the motions of my good-byes with Ella May. The poor slob's got a bad back."

"Her front's no better."

Marti laughed. "I'm glad I can still see what I once saw in you, and, buster, that's a compliment. File it for future reference." She walked away, blithely swinging the duffel bag. His eyes followed her until she disappeared into the hotel. He dwelled for a while on what their marriage might have been had either one of them been smarter about managing the other. And then he realized he was wasting precious time.

An hour later, the Renault was parked across the street from Karen Frost's apartment house. Miraculously, there had been no sign of the white Thunderbird from the moment he left the hotel. It almost gave him a feeling of rejection, as though Gucci and Hayes had grown bored with him and decided to catch a movie instead. Or did they know Marti? Had they recognized her when she left the hotel and decided to switch trails. Were they smart enough to make their own decisions? He doubted that. They had to know he'd be at Hagar Simon's later. Whoever was paying their expense account might have decided to save on gas.

Norton scanned the stree for a sign of a plainclothesman. Further up the street he saw a blue Volvo parked in the driveway of a ranch style house that had a FOR RENT sign planted in the front garden. A man sat behind the wheel reading a paperback. Norton left the Renault and locked it. He saw the man in the Volvo glance in his direction as he started to cross the street. Norton resisted the urge to give him the boy scout sign. He entered the building and pressed Karen Frost's buzzer. He waited and then pressed it again. She had to be at home. He left the building and crossed to the blue Volvo. The man behind the wheel saw him approaching and placed the paperback on the seat next to him. He had the look of a cop, but then lots of people had that nowadays.

"Hi," said Norton with a friendly grin, using caution, in case the man might be a real estate agent awaiting a prospective tenant and not who he hoped he was. "I see this place is for rent."

"That's what the sign says." His attitude was friendly, and Norton didn't miss the bulge under the left arm of his jacket. He was who he hoped he was.

"I'm Norton Valentine."

The man's face brightened. "Thought you might be. Sparks gave me pretty good description." Norton thought his voice chords might have recently been sandpapered. "He left out your dimples. My name's Grafton. Abe Grafton."

"How long you been on?"

"Got here about an hour ago."

It was more than three hours since Sparks had suggested putting a guard on Karen Frost. "What took you so long?"

"They're short-handed at the station. This should be my day off. I wasn't home when Ira phoned. Took me a while to get here."

"I see. Somebody covering the back of the place?"

"Hank Rosen's parked in the garage under the building. There's no back way out. The tenants either come out the front door or go down to the garage. We came out here together."

"Then she's still inside."

"Should be. There was a doorman on when we got here. He said she was in."

"He's not there now."

Grafton shrugged. "He could be any place inside, I guess. I didn't see him go off. Her car's still parked in the garage. It's a Jap job. A red Toyota."

"I've been buzzing her. She doesn't answer."

Grafton shrugged again. "Maybe she vants to be alone."

"Got any keys on you?"

"Always do." Grafton reached into his trouser pockets and handed Norton a set of skeleton keys. Norton returned to the building and buzzed Karen Frost again. He leaned on the bell until the tip of his finger turned white. There was still no response. He let himself into the lobby and looked around for the doorman. There was no sign of life, and the lobby was as silent as a church after mass. He went down the hall past the elevator to Karen Frost's door. He pressed the buzzer there and then banged on the door. He pressed his ear to the door, but heard nothing. He let himself into the apartment.

"Karen?" He shut the door and entered the living room repeating her name. "Karen?" He crossed to the kitchen and then retraced his steps across the living room to the bedroom. He opened the door and went in.

She was lying on the bed in a foetal position. She was wearing a thin housecoat and apparently nothing else. Her eyes were open and milky with death. Her right hand was hidden under her body, but her left was exposed and outstretched. Norton felt for her pulse, knowing it was a vain gesture. There was a scratch mark in the crook of her elbow, as though she might have done battle with an insect or been mainlining. He examined her arm for any telltale syringe punctures but could find none. On the nightstand, he saw an empty glass and a bottle with a chemist's label that probably had contained sleeping pills. Norton wrapped a handkerchief around the bottle and sniffed it. It told him nothing. He replaced the bottle and stared at the dead woman's face. This wasn't the face that Clay Stopley had admired and loved. The bruise on her right eye seemed even uglier than it had looked the previous day. She had obviously not bothered to make up that morning. There were dark circles under her eyes, and her lips seemed shriveled and pinched. There was only one hope left for renewing some semblance of her beauty, a skilled mortician.

Norton opened closets and drawers and swiftly and skillfully examined their contents. He repeated the operation in the sitting room, bathroom and kitchen, but he found nothing that would be of any use to him. He couldn't shake a feeling someone had preceded him in these actions. He could find nothing that linked her to Hagar Simon or Clay Stopley. He found nothing that linked her with anything but an impersonal existence. He pocketed his handkerchief and left the apartment. In the lobby he found the doorman. He was a slightly built man with Mexican features wearing a new, but ill-fitting, uniform. He was rocking on his heels with his arms folded, humming atonally while staring mindlessly out the glass door. He sensed Norton's approach and quickly stood stiffly, touching his cap politely with two fingers, parting his lips in a menial smile that displayed a row of crooked, tobacco-stained teeth. Norton at last found a use for the private operative's license he was carrying. He pulled out his wallet, jerked it open, and flashed the ticket under the doorman's face. The man scanned it rapidly and made a wheezing noise. His eyes became wary, and whatever it was he had to hide didn't interest Norton.

"You know Karen Frost?"

"Yeah. Sure. Down the hall behind you." A Brooklyn Mexican, decided Norton.

"What time did you start work this morning?"

"A little after eight. Why?"

"Did you notice if Miss Frost had any visitors?"

"I don't think so." There was a Latin lilt to the reply. "I mean she might have. I have to go off the post every so often. You know, do an errand for one of the tenants, take a leak, things like that. There's supposed to be two of us on duty, but we're short-staffed, you know?" He regarded Norton quizzically. "Something wrong?"

"Something's wrong." He went outside and waved frantically at Abe Grafton. Grafton left his car and arrived at a sprint. Norton told him about Karen Frost. They entered the building, and Grafton sent the doorman down to the garage to get Hank Rosen. Then he followed Norton back to Karen's apartment. Norton went to the phone while jerking a thumb toward Karen's bedroom. Grafton went there, and Norton dialed Ira Sparks. While he was waiting to be connected, a six-foot cherub entered the apartment, puffing. Hank Rosen had the kind of seraphic face that belonged on a birthday card. He was probably in his late twenties but looked sixteen and unkissed.

"Who're you?" he asked Norton in a piccolo voice that made farce comedy of the stern look on his face.

"Norton Valentine. Grafton's in the bedroom. Karen Frost's dead." Ira Sparks had come on the phone. "Ira? Valentine here. I'm at Karen Frost's. She's dead." Rosen joined Grafton in the bedroom while Norton heard Sparks explode at the other end. "Hold your fire, Ira. Grafton tells me he and his partner only came on an hour ago. She looks and feels as though she's been dead longer than that." He went testy. "No, I didn't grope, but I felt for her pulse, and rigor mortis has set in." He listened. Then he said, "It looks like an overdose of sleeping pills, but I wouldn't say positively. Well . . . her eyes are open. When you o.d. on pills, you usually shut them and go bye-bye. See you soon." He hung up as Grafton and Rosen entered from the bedroom. "Ira's on his way."

Rosen tweetled to Grafton, "He'll chew our asses for this."

"Ira's a vegetarian," replied Grafton. "Looks to me like she was out before we got here."

"I'm with you," said Norton. He watched them as they began searching the apartment. He wondered if they knew what they were looking for or just keeping busy until Sparks arrived. Then he thought of Marti. He wanted her to know about Karen before she heard it on the air or read it in a newspaper. He wanted to tell her he didn't believe she'd committed suicide, that some other means had been used to dispatch her to hooker heaven. He wanted to tell her to be careful and watch her step, because maybe whoever put it to Karen might know Marti had ministered to her Tuesday morning and might have heard something incriminating.

Don't you waste that energy on me.

It isn't a waste of energy, sweetheart, it's the Rover Boy to the rescue. Murder is never neat, but there's an unusually sloppy killer on the loose. The empty glass and pill bottle are a classic touch, but I have a hunch an autopsy will tell another story. The murderer should have remembered to shut Karen's eyelids. He was in too much of a hurry. Much too much of a hurry. Maybe right now he's sitting somewhere with a hamburger and a cup of coffee and in his mind retracing his act and realizing where he bungled. Maybe he's on a bench in Griffith Park staring at the spot where he dumped Clay Stopley. Maybe he's two guys doing a Laurel and Hardy act in the front seat of a white Thunderbird. That might explain their sudden dereliction of duty the past few hours.

"Anything?" Grafton asked Rosen.

"Nothing," tweetled Rosen. They sat on the couch and looked at Norton, who was posed on the chair near the telephone like Rodin's *Thinker*.

"Mr. Valentine." Norton turned to Grafton. "You didn't give this place a fast once over before calling us, did you?"

Norton said he hadn't and wondered how to contact Marti. He wanted to kick himself for not thinking of asking her for her phone number at the swimming pool. It was too emotional a confrontation for a minor matter like that, he thought ironically.

Ella May Rudge.

He reached for the phone and dialed the hotel. He asked for Ella May Rudge. Hank Rosen reacted to her name. "Ella May Rudge, the *singer*. You *know* her?"

Norton was astonished. "Don't tell me you've heard of her?"

"I've got every album she's ever made. She's got the voice of an angel."

"Have you ever seen her?"

"Not in person," said Rosen dreamily.

"Don't, and keep your illusions." Into the phone, he said, "Ella May? Norton Valentine. No, no . . . it's not about a massage . . ." Rosen and Grafton exchanged glances. "I lost Marti's phone number. I was wondering if you had it." She said she'd go look, and he waited. In the distance he could hear the police siren heralding the advent of Sparks and company. The two plainclothesmen got to their feet and busied themselves looking busy. They were badly in need of direction as they renewed looking into closets and drawers. Ella May was back on the phone, and Norton was prepared with address book and pen. She was repeating the number slowly, and he wished somebody was standing behind her with an electric prod. "You're a sweetheart, Ella May. Thanks a million. What? I won't forget. The minute I feel tense, I'll send you a signal. 'Bye now." He hung up as Ira Sparks came charging into the apartment followed by Boyd Gross and Maurice Mosk. Mosk carried his little black bag in his right hand; in his left, he held a pear he was rapidly demolishing. There were no greetings exchanged, although Boyd Gross waved his hand lightly in Norton's direction. Grafton and Rosen led the others to the corpse.

Norton realized this was not the time to phone Marti. Sparks would certainly question why Norton was taking special pains to alert her.

"What brought you here this time?" He hadn't heard

Sparks return to the living room. The big man was remarkably light on his feet. Norton stood up while pocketing the address book and pen.

"I thought of some more questions to ask her, naturally."

"Naturally. What time did you phone her?"

"I didn't. I decided to come straight over. Even if I had phoned, I don't think she would have been in any condition to answer. I think she's been dead two or three hours. Mosk can tell us if I'm right about that." He followed Sparks back to the bedroom. The coroner was still examining the body. Norton crossed and stood behind Mosk. "Is it an o.d.?"

Mosk looked over his shoulder at Norton. "Well, there's the bottle and the glass, but I can't give you a positive answer until I perform the autopsy. That's a pretty ugly right eye she's got."

"She got that a couple of days ago," contributed Boyd Gross.

"I can tell that myself," growled Mosk. "But it might have been concussed. From the pallor of her skin and the condition of her pupils, I detect signs of some sort of shock to her system." He was examining the scratch on her left arm Norton had detected earlier. "Hmmm." Mosk applied his thumbs to the scratched area and stretched the skin. "Looks like a puncture there."

Sparks leaned over for a close look. "She might have been a junkie."

"Might," said Mosk, "but I don't see any signs of any other syringe marks."

"Maybe she was just beginning," offered Gross. Hank Rosen snickered, and Ira Sparks shot him a filthy look. Two morgue attendants arrived carrying a stretcher. Mosk motioned them to wait while he continued examining the scratch. Then he shook his head and straightened up with an expression of pain. "My back's killing me." He waved at the attendants. "Wrap her, and file her. I'll ride back with you."

Norton returned to the living room, followed by Sparks and Gross. "It was a good idea to give her some protection,

Ira, but I guess it was a little too late."

Sparks was wiping sweaty palms with a bandanna handkerchief. "That's what stinks about this job. Not enough men available. It took 'em over an hour to round up Grafton and Rosen." He stopped Mosk who was heading through the living room toward the front door. "Maurice, how long would you say she's been croaked?"

"About two to three hours, maybe longer. I'll know better later." He continued out.

Sparks said to Norton, "Any chance you're going to tell me what you were going to ask Frost?"

"Sure," said Norton. "I was going to ask her if she saw Clay Stopley murdered."

"What makes you think she did?"

"Her black eye, among other things." He headed for the door. He glanced at his wristwatch and said, "I'll phone you later for the autopsy report. Oh, by the way, I seem to have lost Tom Gucci and Vince Hayes. You didn't warn them off me by any chance?"

Sparks stuck his thumbs in his belt. "You told me it wasn't worth the bother."

"I know. But I wondered if they might have been called off me long enough to take care of Miss Frost." The attendants were crossing the room, carrying the covered stretcher.

Sparks said, "I'll ask them about that." He spoke to Gross. "Have them brought in." Gross crossed to the telephone to dial headquarters. Norton followed the stretcher-bearers into the hall. He didn't for one moment think that the two hoods were responsible for Karen Frost's death, but he thought the suggestion to Sparks might meet with Boyd Gross's approval. The doorman held open the door for the morgue attendants. Norton spoke to the man as he passed him. "Better let your bosses know there's another apartment available."

8

Boyd Gross was behind the wheel of the police car, returning to the station house. Ira Sparks was holding the microphone of the shortwave hookup to the station, relaying the order to pick up Tom Gucci and Vince Hayes for questioning. Grafton and Rosen were on their way home to make the most of what was left of their day off. Sparks replaced the microphone on its hook and then sat back with his hands on his knees. He seemed oblivious to the uncomfortable perspiration on his forehead and upper lip. There was a dreamy, faraway look in his eyes which Boyd Gross saw reflected in the windshield, and Gross wondered if he was off in Morocco or Tanganyika or maybe somewhere in South America. His mind should be on these murders, thought Gross. *You think there might be more?* Boyd could hear his own incredulous-sounding voice asking Norton that question at lunch. Of course, there might be more, Gross realized, and cursed himself for not trying to press Norton further. Clay Stopley was murdered at Hagar Simon's castle, and Karen Frost had been his special girl friend, and girls like Karen have other girl friends, and sometimes they share confidences, which means the murderer might have an additional cast of characters to worry him. Karen either saw the murder committed or had a pretty fair guess as to the identity of the killer. The killer was taking no chances on her promised silence under the duress of a beating and eliminated her. Karen must have an address book or possibly a diary, and there was no sign of either at her apartment. He voiced all this to Ira Sparks, who surfaced from his reverie with a troubled look.

"I been thinking along the same lines," said Sparks gruffly. "Now, if I could find out who Karen Frost's been buddy-buddy with . . ."

"Stands to reason they be among Hagar Simon's regulars."

"Stands to reason, all right." He was agitating his hands against his thighs. Gross wondered if it was only these murders troubling him. "I'm almost tempted to subpoena Valentine for the information he's withholding."

"Fat lot of good that would do you. His L.A. office would kill it before the ink was dry."

"I'd like to beat it out of him. Don't give me one of your tender looks. That's how I feel, and I don't give a dead hump who knows it. I know, I know . . . if Stopley hadn't been a Fed, the case would have been left to us. But he was a Fed, and the Feds look after their own. Well, Karen Frost was just a plain civilian, and she belongs to us. Let little Norton try to stick his two cents in where *she's* concerned." He now sat with his arm across the back of the seat behind Boyd Gross. "You like that bastard, don't you?"

"Valentine? What's to dislike?"

"I mean, you admire him." The challenge in Sparks's voice spelled trouble. Boyd Gross wondered if he dared crash into the car ahead of them. "Well, you do, don't you?"

"Is it illegal?"

"I didn't ask for any smartass lip. What's to admire in him?"

"He's not afraid to die."

Sparks detonated. "That's a reason to admire him? You afraid to die? Am I afraid to die?"

"That's not what I'm saying. I think Valentine's sticking his neck out above and beyond the line of duty. He had the courage to blow his cover and blow it fast and set himself up as the bait to get the kind of nibbles he needs."

"Big deal! What makes you think he's working alone? He's probably got half his L.A. bureau covering him right now."

"He may call them in in time, but I doubt if he has them now. Why send him out from the East? Why not pick someone from their local force? Because he's a specialist, that's why. Top grade."

"And for that you admire him?" Sparks's voice was flat and filled with disappointment.

"I couldn't do his job. I can't think the way he thinks. And any man who's got it over me, I admire. I admire short order cooks."

"You give me a pain in the ass. You got too much education."

Boyd Gross couldn't wait to repeat this conversation to his wife.

Thank you for *caw*-ling. Malibu Mistral."

Norton thought the switchboard operator had said "Malibu Mistrial" as he asked for Marti Leigh.

"Marti Leigh? I'm ringing Marti Leigh."

Norton sat on the couch in his living room, tapping his foot impatiently. His shirt was sticky with sweat and clinging to his skin. He reached over and slid back the door leading to the swimming pool. A lone male bather was floating in the water, his long wet beard trailing like fetid seaweed.

"Yes?" Marti sounded half-asleep.

"It's Norton. I got your number from Ella May. I'll make this quick." He told her about Karen. If he had the results of her autopsy before leaving to pick up Lila Frank, he'd try to let Marti know.

"If you know, you can call me at Hagar's."

"Why didn't you tell me you were going to be there tonight?"

"I didn't know till I got back. There was a message to call Czardi. I can cancel if you prefer."

"Don't cancel. I like having you where I can keep an eye on you."

"Now, Norton, have you any real reason to think I might be in danger?" She was working too hard on a jocular tone. Norton could sense she was frightened.

"Do you know if Karen kept a diary?"

"I don't. She might have. Why?"

"I frisked her place before calling the police. No address book, no letters. No ashes in either of her fireplaces. Maybe there was a diary, and maybe there wasn't. But an address book had to exist, and I should think she would have had a date book."

"She did have that. She was always making a note of appointments. She always scribbled down who she saw and when she saw them."

"Let's hope she was too upset at the time to scribble you down for Tuesday morning."

"Thanks for the kind thought." The line seemed to go dead.

"*Marti?*"

"I'm here. I'm here. I was just thinking about something. She probably has some family someplace, but I haven't the vaguest idea where . . . I mean . . . what about her funeral? Who'll take care of that?"

"Perhaps Hagar will do the right thing."

"That's almost funny."

"Don't worry about it now. It'll be in the newspapers tomorrow. Some relative might spot it and come forward. Marti, I want you to spend some time thinking hard about Tuesday morning at Karen's. Anything you remember she told you. *Anything*. Some hint, some little description of the bastard who hit her. That's who killed her. That's who killed Clay." He wanted to add, but didn't: And that's who might try to kill you and a dumb little bunny named Viola Pickfair, who spent time with Karen Frost yesterday. And anybody else she might have seen and spoken to since Tuesday morning.

"I'll work hard at it, Nortie. See you later." She hung up. Norton replaced the phone on the receiver and dialed his L.A. office. He repeated his information on Karen Frost. The office instructed him to apprise Ira Sparks of the possible danger to Marti and Viola. Norton suggested in Viola's case it might be expedient to turn her over to her Aunt Chloe for safekeeping. His associate on the other end wondered if he could join Viola. Norton called him a dirty old man and hung up. He referred to his address book and phoned Viola. He got an answering service and left his name and number. He went down the addresses and telephone numbers supplied to him by Ira Sparks and dialed Chloe Jupiter.

Horace X.'s rich baritone told him, "Miss Chloe Jupiter's residence."

"Horace, this is Norton Valentine. Is Miss Jupiter available?"

"She's in the middle of her yoga exercise, Mr. Valentine."

"This is very urgent. It concerns her niece."

"Ah, yes. One moment, Mr. Valentine. I'm putting you on hold."

Norton struggled out of his shirt while waiting. He kicked off his moccasins and wriggled his toes. He loosened his trousers and lit a cigarette, and then Chloe Jupiter came on the phone.

"Why, hullo there, Norton." The sexy, dulcet tones caressed his ears like the practiced blandishments of a geisha girl. "What's all this about Viola?"

Seated on her heart-shaped bed in her purple and gold bedroom, Chloe Jupiter listened to Norton with a troubled face. Horace X. sat on the sofa watching her while doing a cat's cradle with Irving the gorilla. It was Irving's turn, and he was delicately lifting the strings from Horace's fingers to form an intricate design.

"Why, of course uh'm disturbed, Norton. Uh'm so unstrung, uh may have to send fer muh mandolin player." She got to her feet slowly. "Uh'll send muh boys for Viola immediately. Anybody harms a hair of her head will have tuh answer tuh me puhsonally. Uh'll blow the whole works. Gimme the name of yuh hotel. Uh'll be in touch if there's any problem." She listened for a moment. "Yuh'll be at Hagar's later. Make a note of that, Horace. Norton, yuh look out for yuhself. Yuh playin' with fire. Uh don't want yuh tuh get singed in the wrong places." She hung up. "Horace! Get a couple of the boys up from muh puhsonal gymnasium in the basement and go get Viola and bring her here. Make shuah she packs an overnight bag. And, Irvin', put that solid gold string back in muh jewel case 'n' go outside 'n' jog."

Norton phoned Ira Sparks, but was told he was out of the office. He asked for Boyd Gross and was finally connected with him in the morgue. He told him of the possible danger to Marti and Viola. "Viola's aunt is moving her out to her place. She'll be safe there."

"I'll put Grafton onto Marti Leigh," said Boyd. "I've got the autopsy report on the Frost girl. You were right. She didn't o.d. There wasn't enough nembutal in her to kill her. There were traces in her mouth, throat and lungs, which indicates whatever she imbibed was forced into her. She was killed by an air bubble. An empty syringe injected into the crook of her left elbow. The shock was instant and killed her."

"Christ," whispered Norton. "Has Sparks heard this report?"

"Not yet. He's out of the office on something else. Tom Gucci and Vince Hayes haven't been picked up yet either. We're having a very bad day around here."

"Sometimes bad days turn out to be the best."

"Maybe for you." He lowered his voice. "Sparks is on the warpath. You may find him a bit troublesome from here on in."

"I was expecting it. It'll be handled. Please get after Abe Grafton. Marti's at the Malibu Mistral. I spoke to her half an hour ago. Then she's being escorted to Hagar Simon's tonight by Mickey Czardi. Grafton ought to pick up on her somewhere between the two spots."

"Going to let her know she's getting a guardian angel?"

"Yes. To relieve her anxiety. Speak to you later." He hung up and dialed Marti's hotel. This time Marti's "Yes?" was more annoyed than inquisitive. He had a feeling she was not alone.

"Sorry to disturb you again, sweetheart, but you've just won yourself a private watchdog."

Her voice was up several octaves. "What are you talking about?"

"I'm talking about a preventative measure. I've had the police assign a plainclothesman to keep an eye on you."

"Does he do windows?"

"This is for your own safety, Marti. If Karen made a note in her appointment book about your visit Tuesday morning, you could be on the spot. This killer is panicking. He's working overtime to cover his tracks. He's struck twice, and he'll do it again if he thinks he has to. He's playing the odds against being caught. Even if he's nabbed, he knows they can only gas him once."

"I'm thinking I just might pack my bags and get out of here."

Norton was positive he heard a sound of surprise coming from a second party with Marti. "Is somebody with you?"

"Viola's here."

Norton sighed with relief. "Thank God for small favors. Tell Viola I want her to drive to her aunt immediately and stay there. Don't repeat what I'm about to tell you or that little nitwit might take a dive out the window."

"She won't. She's afraid of heights."

Viola was sitting spread-legged with her back to Marti's dressing table. Her eyes and cheeks were blotched with tears, and she was wringing a handkerchief like a silent screen heroine in distress. She was certainly afraid of heights, and being the only other person in the room with Marti, she decided Marti was referring to her. She cocked her head like an inquisitive canary, anxious to find out why Marti was telling whoever it was she was speaking to that Viola was afraid of heights. Viola was afraid of a lot of things from the moment Marti had told her Karen Frost was dead. She was afraid of her aunt and the police and Norton Valentine and why Marti had been pressing her to try and remember as much as possible of her conversation with Karen yesterday.

Marti now knew Viola was another potential victim. She was listening to Norton suggest off the top of his head that she accompany Viola to Chloe Jupiter's. He would call the police station and have Boyd Gross apprise Abe Grafton of Marti's destination. He'd get back to Chloe and tell her to expect both women.

"Well, if you say so, I suppose it's as good an alternative as taking it on the lam," Marti said to Norton halfheartedly.

"You'll be perfectly safe at Chloe's. Now the two of you get moving."

"Wait a minute! I have to tell Czardi!"

"Do it fast, and for God's sake, get a move on!"

Marti winced at the sound of the phone being slammed on the receiver at the other end. She replaced hers and snapped her fingers at Viola. "On your toes, Viola, we're going to your Aunt Chloe's."

"Aunt Chloe? Was that Aunt Chloe you were talking to? Has she asked us to dinner and maybe she's invited a lot of important people who could help me in my career . . ."

She cascaded onward, while Marti wished she had a suture for the chatterbox's mouth.

"Well, what are you packing all that stuff for? Are you spending the weekend? I didn't know you were that friendly with Aunt Chloe because Aunt Chloe doesn't have any women friends not because she doesn't like women but she says most of the women in this town belong to car pools and who are you phoning *now*?"

Norton was busy on his phone to relay the necessary information to Chloe Jupiter and Boyd Gross. He spoke to Chloe first.

"But muh boys have already left for Viola's!" She tapped one foot impatiently while Norton explained. "Well, uh suppose they'll be okay gettin' here. There's safety in numbers, yuh know. Uh'll send someone after Horace X."

Marti was getting a hard time from Czardi. She could envision his sweaty body trembling with aggravation.

"You can't do this to Hagar!" he shouted, "You can't do this to me! You owe us both! She needs you there tonight!"

"Will you shut up and listen!" yelled Marti. "Karen Frost is dead! She's been murdered!"

In the baroque living room of his apartment above his restaurant, Miklos Czardi moved back in shock against a fragile end table and sent a framed, autographed photograph of Zsa Zsa Gabor crashing to the floor. "You must be mad!" he gasped. "You must be utterly mad! Not Karen! Why would anyone kill Karen?! He was wiping his brow with the sleeve of his velvet dressing gown. Marti was talking rapidly and none of it seemed to make much sense to him. Then she disconnected abruptly and he heard the dial tone. He stared at the receiver in his hand as though it had irreparably insulted him. How dare a common chippie hang up on royalty?! How dare anyone cancel him at the last minute?! "Off with her head!" he shouted at a painting of the late Queen Marie of Rumania hanging over his fireplace, and even she seemed to be smirking.

Karen Frost? Murdered?

His finger fumbled at the telephone dial. His hand was palsied with shock and confusion. His finger kept slipping, and he had to hang up twice and redial. Finally he got through to Lila Frank. "Lila! Lila! Have you heard? The most terrible news! Karen Frost has been *murdered!*"

Norton was having his own troubles with the telephone. Boyd Gross was not in his office. Boyd Gross was not in the morgue. He wasn't with Ira Sparks. Ira Sparks wasn't back yet. Did he wish to leave a message? Yes, he wished to leave a message and left it. He slammed the phone down, wriggled out of his trousers and flung them on a chair. Abe Grafton would have to suffer the wild goose chase out to Marti's hotel. He hoped Marti and Viola were on their way to Chloe's. His wristwatch told him there was still a little time to spare before showering and dressing to get to Lila Frank's by eight. He switched on the television set, and into view flicked a grandfatherly gentleman exhorting the elderly to avail themselves of his cut-price dental service. Norton lit a cigarette and tried to compose his thoughts.

There was so much nagging at his brain. His built-in shrew of logic was scolding away, exhorting him to find the logical progression of the clues he had that would lead him to the murderer. Things he had seen, things he had heard and filed away in his brain, little nuggets crying for refining and polishing, to be strung together into a fatal noose. There was too much sidetracking him. Karen's murder. The threat of death hanging over Marti and Viola. Ira Sparks's growing animosity toward him. His top priority should be the cracking of the Hagar Simon assignment. But his instinct was also telling him these parallel lines would suddenly verge and meet at a common junction. Both cases would fuse and explode together. Karen Frost's death might be a blessing in disguise. It could cause a chain reaction that might detonate in his favor. A firework lighting up the sky and spelling out the answers. What was it he knew that was more important than he realized when he heard it?

What the hell's that carnival absurdity on the television screen? The soundtrack was blaring "The Saber Dance," and a beautiful comet wearing the briefest of costumes of spangles and rhinestones and peacock feathers was flashing across a frozen lake wearing shocking pink ice skates. Her hands were gracefully outstretched as she pirouetted into the air and performed a *tour jeté* that brilliantly dissolved into a breath-catching arabesque. She landed on the tips of her skates and held a pose that was caught in closeup by an adoring cameraman, and Norton remembered here was Hagar Holt Simon at the height of her beauty. Then there was a quick cut to a long shot, as the music rearranged into mass hysteria, and the beauteous Hagar was surrounded by two dozen cossacks on skates brandishing sabers, converging on her from all directions, as she nimbly flitted among them and ice chips flew, reminding Norton it was time to pour himself a drink.

"You're drunk!" Lila Frank shrieked into the phone. "You haven't heard one word I told you!"

Burton Hartley glared at the phone he was holding, licked his lips, and said, "I heard every word. I am shocked. I am shocked to hear Karen is dead, and I am shocked to hear you accuse me of being non compos mentis at this early hour of the evening." He was amazed and pleased at his clarity of speech. At his elbow was his third scotch and water, and he could still savor the taste of the bottle of claret he had treated himself to at lunch. "Does Hagar know?"

"I just phoned her!" Lila sounded like a calliope with a full head of steam. "She's taking a goddamn bubble bath and'll have to call me back. I certainly wasn't relaying *that* message through one of her flunkies. *Down*, Shirley! *Heel*, Seymour!" Her Airedales were enjoying a tug of war with her negligee. "Goddamn mutts . . . Burton, are you *listening?*"

"Yes, you called me a goddamn mutt."

"Not you, you drunken sot!"

"That's a redundancy."

"So are *you!*"

How well I know, thought Hartley, as he lifted his glass and sipped.

"I can hear the ice cubes!" yelled Lila.

"Lila, my dearest," murmured Hartley, "why don't you grab me by the hair and take me away from all this? Why are you wasting breath with excoriations? Did you expect me to be sober? Did you expect me to burst into tears at your morbid news? I don't give a damn about Karen Frost. Why should I? What's she to me, or me to Hecuba?"

"Who's Hecuba?"

"Oh, go away, Lila. Go away, and ponder your sins. Do anything you like. I'm out of this. This morning I did the bravest act of my life. I tendered my resignation to the newspaper."

"Burton!"

"I sent a carbon copy to our syndicate. I am now composing my farewell column. I am using prose more purple than my past. Like an old general, I am fading away. I am finished. Kaput. I thought this out carefully in a briefly sober moment in my bath this morning, and for the first time without the fear of someone pulling the plug. I ate a lavish lunch at Scandia without fear of indigestion and washed it down with a piquantly presumptuous bottle of California claret."

"Why didn't you talk this over with me first?" She was flinging her mules at the dogs.

"In a way, I was trying to do that last night. But somehow, it came out all wrong. You've become much too intimidating, Lila. Your fanatical single-mindedness leaves room for nothing else. You've even forgotten we once shared what I look back upon as a rather delightful grand passion."

"That was no grand passion!" Her eyes were ablaze, and her nostrils flared. The dogs had each retrieved a mule and now begged at her feet for a reward, with tails wagging. "It wasn't even good. It just killed time."

He said softly, "I prefer to remember it my way. Now perhaps we should hang up. Hagar may be trying to get through to you."

"I wish I could get through to *you*."

"You have. Believe me, you have." He hung up.

"Burton! *Burton!*" Furiously, Lila jiggled the hook. "Burton, don't you dare hang up on me!" The dogs were whining for attention. "You monsters!" She slammed the phone down and began chasing the dogs around her bedroom. "You know what those goddamn mules *cost?!*"

Marti's hands were tight on the wheel of her yellow

Chrysler convertible. A green scarf knotted under her chin kept her hair in place. The speedometer held at a moderate forty, as she carefully maneuvered the hairpin curves of Malibu Canyon. Beside her sat Viola, whimpering with fear at the sight of the sheer drop she could see to the right of her.

"Oh, Marti, why did you go this way!"

"Because there's less traffic. Will you relax!"

"I can't. You know I'm afraid of heights! I should have driven my own car! I could have gone my own way and met you at Aunt Chloe's."

"Your car's perfectly safe where it is."

"Why are we really going to Aunt Chloe's? Who were you talking to on the telephone back in your room? What's going on? I'm frightened! Tell me what's going on!"

"It's better you don't know."

Viola shifted and faced Marti. "Karen was killed because she knew something about Clay Stopley's murder. That's what it's all about, isn't it?"

Marti shook her head yes and said, "We'll be safe at your Aunt Chloe's."

"Safe from what?" Viola's voice might have come from an echo chamber.

"Oh, Christ, Viola. Why shouldn't I tell you? Whoever killed Karen thinks she might have told either one of us something incriminating about him."

"What's incriminating mean?"

"Oh, Jesus wept."

"Watch out for that curve!"

"Shut up, Viola. I see it." She also saw a car coming up on them in the rearview mirror. It was a red Toyota. She recognized the make. Karen Frost owned one just like it. The idiot in the Toyota was coming at them like a bat out of hell.

"Why are you going faster!" yelled Viola, hanging on to her seat belt.

"There's a bastard gaining speed on us back there. Goddamn! The maniac's going to try and pass us!"

• • •

— 130 —

Norton left the television set on as he carried his drink into the bathroom. He set it down on the sink and tested the hot water in the shower. When he adjusted it to a suitable temperature, he took a sip of the drink, stuck his tongue out at himself in the mirror, then set the drink down again, and removed his undershorts. He stepped under the shower, reached for the soap, and began working up a lather. The music from the television set suddenly increased in volume, and Norton decided another of Hagar's production numbers was underway. He soaped his body and face vigorously and neither heard nor saw the door to the shower stall opening.

In a shockingly swift movement, a towel was flung around his face nearly suffocating him. He dropped the soap and lifted his hands in a lightning movement, but the lightning never had a chance to strike. His hands were grasped and pulled behind him in an agonizing grip. A kick to his ankle sent an electric pain through his system, and his knees buckled. He received a sledgehammer blow to his kidney and then another and then another, and he could not cry out because the towel around his head muffled any sound he tried to make. Blow after blow battered his torso as the shower water poured down on him. Then the door slid shut, and he collapsed to the floor of the stall. The towel now draped limply, and Norton began to retch.

Viola was paralyzed with fear. Her mouth was agape but her vocal chords were frozen. Marti was maneuvering desperately to keep the convertible in control. The red Toyota was trying to force her off the road. The maniac behind the wheel of the Toyota had the brim of his fedora pulled down masking the upper portion of his face. *Why doesn't a car come from the opposite direction. Please God, send a car from the opposite direction!*

God heard. He sent a car from the opposite direction, just as Marti went hurtling around a curve. The driver of the other car, a pickup truck, was caught unawares. He looked like a teenage boy barely old enough to hold a license. That

9

Hagar Simon, toilette completed, was returning Lila Frank's phone call. She was swathed from shoulders to ankles in a bouffant dressing gown of white egret feathers. She gave the impression of having been submerged in a snow bank. Her face was heavily oiled with a miracle lotion that promised eternal, wrinkle-free beauty. She might have been bobbing for apples in a tub of vaseline. She sat at her dressing table, delicately balancing in her left hand the receiver of a beige-colored Princess telephone. While she was dialing, her eyes were glued to the reflection in the mirror of a portable television screen. She held an amused expression, as she watched herself skating rapidly and frantically on a frozen river. The soundtrack underlined the urgency of her situation with the *William Tell Overture*. She was being pursued by six Nazi officers in a snowmobile. Ahead of her lay the precipice of a frozen niagara. Bullets whizzed past her ears, while one of the Nazi officers, possibly a devotee of Herman Melville, was poised and taking aim with a rather sophisticated-looking harpoon. Somehow in the midst of this peril, Hagar found the audacity to perform a series of exquisite pliés.

Hagar burst out laughing.

"What the hell's so funny?" trumpeted Lila Frank at the other end of the line.

"Me, Lila. They're screening one of my disasters on the telly."

"Well, let's see how funny you find *this*. Karen Frost's dead. She's been murdered." Hagar's grip on the receiver tightened. "I got the news from Czardi. *He* got it from Marti Leigh."

Hagar wiped at the corners of her mouth with a tissue. "How did Marti find out?"

"Czardi didn't ask. She's canceled out on us. Mickey thinks she's gone into hiding somewhere. Damn you, Hagar, who killed Clay Stopley?"

Hagar crumpled the tissue. Her knuckles showed white. Her deadly expression would have caused panic in a day nursery.

"Hagar, *tell me*. We must put a stop to this. This maniac will *destroy* us."

Hagar flung the tissue at the television set. "It's too late, Lila. It's too damned late. The damage is done! I'm canceling tonight. I'm getting out."

"The bloody hell you are. Once you go, the Feds will be swarming all over the place. They'll tear it apart. They'll find everything they need. We need time to clean up. You cancel that party, and Valentine knows he's got us. For once in your life, baby, you're going to give a performance, an Academy Award winner. You're going to be the gracious hostess. You will register the proper emotion for dear, departed Karen. I've got the whole thing figured out. By the time the party's over, I'll have everything organized!"

The party's over now, Hagar told herself. The party was over Monday night. She felt a stab of pain in her chest and gasped.

"Hagar!"

Hagar took a deep breath and responded to Lila. "Stop screaming, Lila. I'll do as you say." She took another breath, and the pain began to ease. "Where will you go? What will you do?"

"Why the hell do I have to go anyplace? I'm staying right here. Nobody's got a thing on *me*. I'm in the clear. I'm perfectly *safe*."

How lucky for you, thought Hagar. How very lucky for you. It's only pawns like Hagar Simon who get moved around the board and then knocked out of the game. Lila was continuing to make noises. "Lila, you're wasting time. We both have a lot to do."

"For God's sake, tell me who killed Stopley!"

"I can't. I won't."

"*Putana!*"

"Call me a whore. Call me anything you like. But one day soon you'll understand why I didn't tell you. And don't labor the issue at the party. You do, and I'll blow the lid off." Lila's invective scorched Hagar's ear. "You heard me!" shouted Hagar. "My deal promised me protection, and by God, I mean to have it. Now get off the phone, and do your job!" She hung up and fumbled with a bottle of nitroglycerine tablets. She popped two in her mouth and waited for the medication to take effect. She could feel the blood returning to her face as she reached for the house phone and pressed a button. It connected to a sentry box. "It's Mrs. Simon. Listen carefully. I want you to double-check every guest against the list I've given you. No one, do you understand, no one is to be admitted to the grounds, unless they can give satisfactory identification." She switched her finger to another button. It connected with the garage. "This is Hagar. Now listen carefully, darling. Fill the tank of my fastest car. Pack something for yourself. Only what's necessary. Don't ask questions. Just do as I tell you. Be ready to leave on a moment's notice. When the party is underway, come to my suite and take my brown suede case down to the car. *Make sure you're not seen*. And, darling, don't forget your passport. Well, where do you think we're heading? South, darling, along with the rest of the birds." She pressed a third button. "Bridget? I'm ready to dress now."

For God's sake, tell me who killed Stopley.

Poor, dear Lila. If only I dared. If only I could name him now without endangering myself. He knows it all, Lila. He knows *everything*. Passion always loosened my tongue in more ways than one. My job is finished now. All our jobs are finished now. I have earned an honorable retirement. I mean to enjoy every minute of it. I shall have my operation and then settle into a blissful existence in Rio with one of the most gorgeous creatures who ever chauffeured a car.

I hope to God we get out of here alive.

She opened the bottom drawer of the dressing table and dug beneath the layers of lingerie. She smiled to herself. The feel of the snub-nosed automatic renewed her confidence.

Norton sat on the bathroom floor, doubled up and embracing himself. The agonizing effort it took to crawl from the shower stall was indescribable. The water continued to cascade from the nozzle, and the steam that filled the room was almost beneficial to his aching body. His breath was coming easier now, and soon he would make the effort to get to his feet. The beating he took was a thoroughly professional one. No ribs fractured. No skin broken. No blood. Face untouched. Just a succession of fierce, hard-knuckled blows to the kidneys. Only the preliminaries. The warning. Lay off. Cool the heat. Get out. Signed, "Sincerely Yours, Tom Gucci and Vince Hayes." He couldn't make a positive identification, the towel around his face had insured that. But it had to be those boys. Gucci, the ex-pug. Gucci, the professional. Gucci, who knew exactly where to place his fists. Nemesis with cauliflowered ears.

Slowly, Norton relaxed his hold on himself. He stared at the white tile floor, bracing himself for any fresh stabs of pain. It wasn't too bad. It wasn't too bad at all. There was just a chance he could make it to his feet if he took it in gradual stages. He carefully made it to his knees and then edged his right hand up the wall until he had a grip on the towel rack.

He took another deep breath and then pulled himself up. Oh, Jesus, what agony! His head began to spin, and he braced himself against the wall. He blinked his eyes rapidly until they focused properly. He shook his head and then exhaled. He took a tentative step and then another, and the pain was nowhere near what he anticipated. He'd be all right. He'd make it fine. He wrapped a towel around his midriff and slowly entered the sitting room. He lowered himself gingerly onto the couch and stared at the sliding door he had pushed back earlier when the room overheated. Smart old Norton. Clever old Norton. Always make it easy for the opposition to come in and beat you up. Ah, dear old Ira Sparks. How you would enjoy this moment. How that craggy face would be wreathed with a smile of self-satisfaction. Well, you deserve it, you dirty old mothergrabber.

Norton found his cigarettes and lighter. He lit up and inhaled and then blew a smoke ring and answered the persistent ringing of the hotel phone. It was Boyd Gross.

"Sorry I took so long getting back to you. I was out getting something to eat."

How nice to know the outside world still functions normally. People still eat. People get murdered. People get beaten up. Business as usual. Even Norton's voice sounded normal to himself. Things were looking up. He told Boyd about sending Marti and Viola to Chloe Jupiter's. Boyd said he'd get a motorcycle cop to alert Grafton. Abe was using his own car. It wasn't equipped with a radio phone. Boyd agreed the girls might be safer with Viola's glamorous aunt. Norton then told him about the beating. Gross reacted with comforting concern. Norton assured him he'd be in shape to accompany Lila Frank to Hagar's party. Not to worry, Boyd, he wouldn't miss it for the world. Yes, said Boyd, Gucci and Hayes were still eluding the dragnet, so undoubtedly they could very well have been the culprits.

"Frost's apartment has been thoroughly dusted and sealed," added Gross. "So far nothing useful, but forensics is staying with it. It'll be on the late television news and in tomorrow's papers, with pictures. Some relative of hers is bound to surface. Maybe some dark horse will come crawling out of the woodwork with some useful information. Would you like me to drop over?"

"No, and thanks." Norton took a deeper drag on the cigarette and filled his lungs, with a mental finger for the Surgeon General. "I have to call my office and then make myself pretty for the party."

"Don't dance."

Norton laughed and hung up. On the turquoise phone he dialed his local office. His conversation duplicated the one with Boyd Gross. The concern from the other end about his beating was a deeper one, however. A decision was made, and a plan evolved. Norton offered no argument. It was now go for broke or nothing. Yes, said Norton, he would carry his service revolver tonight. Yes, he would wear his tuxedo, though the jacket wasn't madras. The suit was one of Jay Press's most stylish. He mustn't forget to pay his bill, now long overdue. He hung up and stubbed out the cigarette. He got up slowly and walked around the room. There was still pain, but nothing he couldn't endure. A drink would help, and he poured himself one. Then he slid the door to the pool shut and locked it. He was starting to dress when the hotel phone rang.

"Norton?" It was Chloe Jupiter, and she sounded as though she had just heard an option drop. "The girls ain't here yet! Uh've got muh boys out scoutin' every road from Malibu. They shoulda been here b'now."

Norton paled. "I'll alert the police."

"If anythin's happened to muh niece, uh tell yuh there'll be no controllin' me. Even Irvin's pacin' the room with a worried look. Uh don't like that. Irvin's psychic. Yuh don't suppose they got into some sort of accident, do yuh?"

"Let me call the police. I'll get right back to you."

The only illumination in Ira Sparks's office was from his desk lamp. His trousers were lowered, and he was shooting insulin into his thigh. Then he leaned with both hands on his desk, waiting for the trembling to stop. He gulped air and wiped his brow with a jacket sleeve. He adjusted his trousers and sat in the swivel chair. He replaced the syringe in its case and put it inside his jacket pocket. He was lighting a cheroot when Boyd Gross knocked on the door and entered.

"Christ, I'm glad you're back."

"Nice to know I was missed. I was beginning to think the department could run itself."

Gross ignored the sarcasm and launched into a detailed report of the events concerning Marti Leigh and Viola Pickfair. Sparks listened with a variety of expressions, none of them pleasant. He cursed himself aloud for having taken the time to see his doctor for a checkup. He cursed the municipal government for providing insufficient funds for the required manpower. He ordered an escalation in the search for Tom Gucci and Vince Hayes and an all-points alert for Marti Leigh and Viola Pickfair. Gross had a strange expression on his face.

"What the hell's the matter with you?" roared Sparks.

"Just thinking of my wife, that's all," said Gross, swiftly. "She'll have to eat another lonely dinner."

"Tough on her!"

Gross returned to his office and phoned Norton. Norton was dressed and ready to leave to pick up Lila Frank. Norton was grateful for Gross's information, and on one point, more than grateful. He rewarded Gross with the inside information of the plan evolved by Norton's local office for later that evening. "It blows tonight," concluded Norton. "It's earlier than scheduled, but it blows. We've got no choice. If anything new turns up, you certainly know where to reach me."

Norton phoned Chloe. He was only able to reassure her the police had ordered the all-points alert for Marti and Viola. Chloe wasn't satisfied. "Uh'm gonna call the governor 'n' get the National Guard. He owes me a favor, y'know." Norton tried to assure her such drastic measures weren't necessary. He asked her to keep in touch with him at

Hagar's. "Uh'll be in touch all right. If anythin's happened to Viola, uh'll be in touch with Hagar puhsonally. She'll wish she'd settled in an igloo in Iceland."

Five minutes later, Norton in the Renault pulled out of the hotel garage. He only referred to the rearview mirror when necessary. He knew there would be no white Thunderbird trailing him now.

The castle felt cold and dank. The great central hall seemed warmed only by the radiance of Hagar wearing a shimmering silver djellaba decorated only by a modest sapphire brooch and matching bracelet. She wafted down the grand staircase, looking like the wraith of a departed Ziegfeld girl, lacking only the melodious accompanying strains of some Irving Berlin walking music to complete the effect. She passed the rows of armor evenly spaced along the stairs, placed there as they had been years ago under the supervising eye of her late husband Isaac. She nodded at her footmen as she casually passed them on her way into the great banquet hall, dazzling in the light emanating from the massive crystal chandelier, which Chloe Jupiter had insisted was stolen from Loew's Pitkin. Butlers, waiters and maids hurried back and forth from the kitchen, bearing salvers of assorted foods. Three bartenders hurried to complete the setting up of their station. Hagar passed among the help, nodding and murmuring approval, and on her way to the kitchen swiped a shelled pistachio nut to nibble on. In the kitchen, she voiced her approval to the chef and his five assistants and felt reassured when the chef patted his breast to indicate his shoulder holster was in place. The chauffeur sat at the kitchen table eating his dinner, and she caught his sly look, which told her orders had been attended to. Hagar's tour of duty took her back to the great hall, where the majordomo was opening the solid oak door to welcome the first guests. A sparrow of an old woman with a face decayed by personal and professional disappointment entered, followed by a swarthy young man with black, lacquered hair.

"I suppose we're the first," crackled the old sparrow.

Hagar went to them with outstretched hands and a professional smile. "Margot darling! You're the first and the most welcome. And Manuel, how dashing you look!" Manuel flashed his ivories as he took one of Hagar's hands and kissed it. The majordomo signaled past the group to someone in the great banquet hall, and a Brahms string quartet flooded the castle from carefully hidden speakers.

Margot parted her shriveled lips and whispered to Hagar, "It's our anniversary. Two weeks today since I brought Manuel up from Tiajuana."

Hagar thought to herself, and they said it wouldn't last.

Perched on a leather stool at the bar in her living room, Lila Frank was cooling her right index finger in a glass of champagne. The digit ached from the excessive amount of dialing she had accomplished since speaking to Hagar. Her vocal chords ached from the shouting they'd been subjected to, but she felt satisfied and confident. Only one call had come through on her private wire, and the news it brought her had filled her with apoplectic fury.

"I told you no rough stuff, you bloody bastard! Since when have you started making your own decisions? So you don't like his face. All right, all right, so I told you not to lay a finger on him! Ahhhhh, you're dumb like the rest of them! Dumb, I tell you, *dumb!*" She then spewed a stream of gutter invective followed by, "Well, you at least had the sense to ditch the car. What do you want for that? A gold star? Where you calling from? Uh huh, that's at least using your head. Well, stay there, and I'll call you later. Listen! *Wait!* He ain't *dead*, is he? *Mama mia*, thank God for that. Do you realize now this whole goddamn affair at Hagar's is a big expensive waste of time? Ahhhh, go stick your head up a pig's ass!"

She glanced at her wristwatch and drained the champagne from the glass. She hopped off the stool and adjusted her red and gold sari. The things she let Jean Louis talk her into. She snatched her gold evening bag from a table and heard the Airedales alternating barks and whines from one of the upstairs bedrooms where they were imprisoned for the night. A car was coming up the drive, and Lila hurried to the door.

Norton stifled a groan as he got out of the Renault and crossed to Lila's front door. As he reached for the gargoyle brass knocker, the door was flung open, and Lila gasped.

Norton remembered his stupid grin. "You look surprised. Did you forget we had a date?"

"Forget?" croaked Lila. She cleared her throat and quickly composed herself. "How could I forget. I'm just surprised you're on time."

"I'm always prompt. You seem a bit distraught."

"I guess I'm still a little spaced out over Karen. That was terrible news. Do you want a drink, or should we head straight for Hagar's?"

"Whatever you say."

"We can drink at Hagar's." She slammed the door shut behind her and preceded him to the car. Norton told her she looked uncommonly beautiful in the sari and hoped she wasn't contemplating suttee.

"What's that?" asked Lila as she slid onto the seat next to the driver's.

"An old Indian custom. They cremate their dead in India. When a husband dies, a wife is expected to join him on the funeral pyre."

"Ain't that a hot one," commented Lila grimly. Norton was getting in behind the wheel. Lila thought she caught an expression of pain. "Something bothering you, Norton?"

"I fell in the shower and hit my back."

Lila folded her hands over the gold evening bag. "I hope it's not too painful."

Norton managed a smile. "I'll survive."

"Yes, I can see you will. Do you know the way to Hagar's from here?"

"Bear right, I should think."

"That's it. Bear right, and follow the yellow brick road. I

hope you don't mind, but we'll have to make an early night of it. I've got a heavy day tomorrow, starting at the crack of dawn. I tape my television show."

"Fine by me. I don't know how long this back of mine will hold up."

"You poor guy. You should have seen a doctor."

"If I don't feel any better in the morning, I'll see one."

"Awful about Karen."

"Awful."

"How'd you hear about it?"

"I found her body."

Lila stared at him. "You have a date with her?"

"No, I just decided to drop by and ask her a few more questions."

Lila settled back in the seat. "You're not really a stockbroker, are you?"

"Not really."

"You a private investigator or something?"

"I'm doing Clay's family a favor. We've known each other a long time. Clay and I were at college together. He was the best man at my wedding."

Don't be dead, Marti. Please don't be dead. It's all I can bear being haunted by Clay. Don't be dead, because I love you, and I want you back. I'm a damn fool to want you back, but that's how it is. I want you back.

"Seems to me you said in the plane you weren't married."

"We were divorced a couple of years ago."

"Why the stockbroker act?"

"People are less suspicious when you're hunting information and invitations. I know Clay was murdered at Hagar's castle."

"You've got positive information?"

"Very positive."

"Who from?"

"That would be telling."

"That's why I'm asking. Don't forget I'm a reporter."

"Heard any good reports lately?"

— 143 —

"You're cute." She snuggled close to him, and the pressure of her body made him wince. "Got any ideas who murdered Clay and Karen?"

Norton pursed his lips, and Lila heard, "Ummmmm."

"What does *that* tell me."

"It tells you, for the moment, my lips are sealed."

Lila moved away from him, opened her purse, extracted a mirror, and surveyed her face in it. "I guess I don't look too bad."

"Where are you from, Lila?"

"Right here."

"I mean what did you do before you became a big celebrity?"

"Worked hard at becoming one."

"You sound ashamed of your background."

"Not at all. It's just very ordinary. If I ever write my memoirs, I'll have to dream up a pack of lies to make them interesting. There's Hagar's."

Smart girl, Lila. Very smart girl. I wish I was wearing a hat, so I could take it off to you. You know I've been beaten up tonight. I could tell from your look of surprise when standing in the doorway. Yet you almost seemed grateful to see me alive and in the flesh. You didn't want me beaten up, because you wanted to bore me with this charade at Hagar's. Well, Lila baby, there's a big surprise in store for you. It's not going to be all that dull an event. There are circumstances now in operation beyond your control. It's not the way we wanted it to happen, but a maniac has forced our hand. We'll all have to make the best of a situation none of us wants. But there are compensations to contemplate. Something worthwhile will come of it. Not the best, but still worthwhile. That's how it is in my business. You aim for the moon but sometimes settle for a satellite.

"Pull up at one of the sentry boxes," ordered Lila. "Hagar has a very tight security. Nobody gets in who isn't on her official list."

•   •   •

On Malibu Canyon Road, where the accident between Marti's yellow Chrysler convertible and the pickup truck had taken place, Horace X.'s motorcycle was now parked. He had come across the telltale skid marks. Now, scrambling down to the valley below in his white jumpsuit and matching white helmet, he looked like a black ghost. The pickup truck was burnt out but still smoldering. In the glare of his flashlight, he saw Marti's upended car. His feet struck rocks and shale causing clouds of dust and a mini-avalanche. He directed his flashlight at the pickup truck. What was behind the wheel looked like a side of charred beef. He swung the flashlight around and saw the doors had been torn loose from the other car. The tree it had connected with was almost uprooted. There was nobody behind the wheel. The body in the passenger seat hung limply, held in place by a safety belt. Horace X. reached the car and recognized Viola. From the angle of her head he could tell her neck was broken. She was heavily cut and bruised, and her face and body was caked with blood. Horace X. cursed aloud and then went looking for the driver. He found Marti some twenty feet away from the car sprawled on her back across some clumps of chapparal. She wasn't a pleasant sight. Blood and dirt almost totally obscured her features. From the way her legs were twisted, Horace X. could tell they were badly broken. He knelt at her side and touched a hand. It was warm. He listened for a heartbeat and heard a faint response. No one had ever scrambled up that ravine with the speed and desperateness displayed by Horace X.

"I've heard so much about you, Mr. Valentine."

Norton held Hagar in his eyes. He was unprepared for the delicate beauty of the lady in person. Here was no steely-eyed harpie, no Medusa to turn him to stone. It was hard for him to believe this soft and voluptuous woman who was greeting him with warmth and friendliness had caulked the seams of her middle-age with corruption and immorality. He would have cast her as the headmistress of an elegant girl's finishing school. He clasped the delicate hand Hagar extended and said, "It's a pleasure meeting you, Mrs. Simon. You look exquisite!"

"Good heavens!" She might have just won the sweepstakes. "Courtly manners in this day and age. You've made my day. May I call you Norton?"

Lila simpered, "And he can call you Hagar, and I'm calling a waiter, because I'm perishing for a drink. Hey, *you* with the tight ass!" She elbowed her way to her quarry, leaving Norton alone with Hagar.

"Don't you find Lila unique?" inquired Hagar melodiously. "She wears her vulgarity like a medal of honor. Is there anyone special you'd care to meet?"

"I've met her."

"You cast a very smooth line, Norton. So you're a friend of Harvey Tripp's. How is Harvey?" Lila returned with two scotches and water and handed one to Norton.

"Harvey Tripp's dead."

Lila almost dropped her glass and blurted, "But his secretary never told Burton . . ."

Hagar's voice bled through Lila's. "But that's terrible! I saw nothing about it in the newspapers."

"It's been kept under wraps pending an investigation. He committed suicide last Saturday. He hung himself. His private papers indicated he was being blackmailed."

"How *awful*," whispered Hagar. Norton could understand why she never made it as an actress. Hagar was addressing Lila. "Death does come in threes, doesn't it. Harvey Tripp, Clay Stopley . . . and dear Karen." She again favored Norton. "We do live in evil times, don't we?"

"I'm sure you're well aware of that."

Hagar quickly looked past him and saw her new arrivals. "Oh there's the Lockwoods! Harry! Virginia! How marvelous to see you! Norton, do excuse me."

"And who," asked Norton of Lila, "are the Lockwoods?"

"V.U.P.'s. Very Unimportant People. They don't even get burglarized. Let's see what's doing in Madison Square Garden." She led the way to the banquet hall.

"Magnificent tapestries," commented Norton.

Lila was caught in the middle of a loud greeting across the vast room to Margot and Manuel. "The Gobelins will get you if you don't watch out."

"It's been said before," replied Norton drily. Scanning the crowded room, he was reminded of a painting by Breughel. Walpurgis night in southern California. Hagar, the stunning witch who probably wouldn't know the difference between a broomstick and a vacuum cleaner. Her hastily assembled guests, extras, bit players and walk-ons, a bizarre potpourri of decadents and innocents, greedily swilling her free liquor and stripping the buffet tables like a plague of destructive beetles. Gossip masquerading as wit, innuendo trespassing as bon mots; gone was a gentler era when ladies dropped their handkerchiefs instead of their brassieres. His innards recoiled with disgust at the sight of shriveled Margot and her young Mexican consort in a kiss so passionate their eyeballs were touching. The music now blaring from the hidden speakers was atonal and existential and offended him with its dissonance, and Lila was tugging impatiently at his sleeve.

"Some party!" she shouted.

"Wow."

"I didn't think you were very impressed." She sipped her drink. "Did Harvey Tripp really hang himself?"

"From a flagpole outside his window. I'm told a dozen people saluted before they realized it was a body."

"Why didn't you tell me about his suicide on the plane?"

"I didn't want you worrying Hagar."

Her eyebrows went up. "Why should it worry Hagar?"

"There's a lot about her in his private papers."

They were standing near open French doors leading to a garden, and a light breeze sent some strands of Lila's hair fluttering across her face. She brushed them aside with a gesture of annoyance, as she said, "I gather you've been privy to those papers."

Norton's smile was not a friendly one. "Why else would I mention them?"

"Maybe to start a little panic around here."

"The panic's already underway. You knew I didn't slip and hurt my back. I was beaten up."

A kaleidoscope of reactions crashed on her face. She opened her mouth to remonstrate, but her tongue seemed glued to her upper palate. She hadn't foreseen such a surprise attack. This man was either the shrewdest under-cover agent in the business or the sort of fool of a daredevil proliferating in paperbacks. She moistened her lips and said, "This some kind of a put-on?"

"You didn't expect me to show up tonight. That look on your face when you opened the door told me that. I didn't get a look at the boys who did the job. They kept a towel around my face. But the guy who did the slugging was a professional. I've suffered enough jabs in my lifetime to know that. His name's Tom Gucci. He works with a smalltime hood named Vince Hayes. What was the point? Wasn't the professional bedlam tonight designed especially for me?"

"What the hell makes you think you're so special?"

"I'm not. I'm Mr. Ordinary himself. But I helped make you think I was special. We don't have to play the game any longer, Lila. We both know this is closing night."

"I need another drink," she said hotly. He grabbed her wrist and pulled her back.

"Don't walk out on me when I'm about to offer you a deal." She pulled her hand free and placed her glass on a table. She made an elaborate business of adjusting her sari.

"Ahhhh, what kind of deal crap? What are you talking about? You're punchy. You got a wet brain in that shower."

"The heat's on, and you've been feeling it ever since Clay Stopley infiltrated Hagar's hospitality."

"I didn't know anything about him! He was just another out-of-town john to me. Don't forget I was in New York when he was murdered."

"You were in New York long enough to brush your teeth." Her jaw dropped. "You spent most of that time in Europe. Shall I tell you under which phony passport you traveled?"

Her eyes were desperately signaling past him for help. She

could see Miklos Czardi and Burton Hartley and caught a quick glimpse of Hagar conferring with a butler, but neither of the three noticed her. She trilled a ridiculous laugh and said, "So I've got a boyfriend stashed away over there. Very important. Very famous. Very married. So we have to make elaborate plans to meet on the sly, that's a Federal case?"

"It might be if the boyfriend's Salvatore Gucci."

"Who?" She repeated the ridiculous laugh. "You got rocks in your head, you know that? Where would I know Salvatore Gucci? He's an old man! I was a kid when he was deported! Ah, come on now, Norton. Don't disappoint me. I thought you were smarter than that. So you've had a tracer on me because Stopley met me at one of Hagar's parties. Whatever you boys think you've got on Hagar, anybody who knows her is suspect. Okay, I buy that. Guilt by association. What the hell! Why would this party be put up special for you? Why would I have you beaten up?"

"This party *was* put on special for me, because there was no party planned when you invited me last night. There's a tight security on all of Hagar's regulars. They didn't get any invitations until this morning by phone. Tom Gucci is Salvatore's grandson. I think you know Tom Gucci."

"*Never* met him in my life." She snarled the sentence like a cornered cat.

"Okay, if that's the way you want it."

"I'm telling it like it *is*."

"You're telling it the way you'd like it to be. I'm telling you you're a liar, and you ought to listen to my deal."

She told him to do something to himself that was physically impossible.

"Not with my bruised ligaments, honey. Lila . . . Harvey Tripp's papers . . . you're mentioned in them. Prominently."

10

Miklos Czardi was bantering with a famous Hollywood agent who hoped he looked like Mark Spitz. The Prince Valiant hairdo and the John Wilkes Booth moustache were a fair approximation, and he was slightly damp, but the blemished sallow skin, the slumped shoulders and the pot belly spoke more of Bacchanalian self-indulgence rather than an Olympic prowess. Czardi was undiplomatically extolling the virtues of a rival agent's major male client. "My dear Oscar," said Czardi, "Burt Douglas can cut any actor down to size."

Oscar growled, "The only actor that bum could cut down to size is Michael Dunn, and he's dead!"

Czardi felt a gentle nudge and turned and saw Burton Hartley. Hartley signaled him with slightly glazed eyes. Czardi excused himself from Oscar and accompanied Hartley out of the agent's earshot. "What's wrong?"

"It looks as though Lila is finding the gentleman she's with somewhat troublesome." Hartley nodded toward the open French doors, and Czardi saw Lila and Norton.

Czardi's eyelids hooded. "That's no gentleman; that's Norton Valentine."

"So *that's* Norton Valentine. He's not at all the way I pictured him. He's handsome enough, but hardly heroic. But then, in these dreadful times, heroes and villains are so interchangeable, it's the era of the chameleon. I want to talk to him. I want to hear more about Harvey Tripp. I've still a few more columns to deliver. I'd love to leave my readers with one last blaze of glory. Doesn't Lila look frantic? I wonder if she made the mistake of asking him to guess her age."

They elbowed their way past two women discussing a celebrated local gigolo.

"I despise that man," said one woman. "He's always taking money from women."

"So is Ohrbach's."

They recognized Czardi and gurgled in his direction. He blew kisses and then averted his face with a grimace.

Lila was saying with defiance to Norton, "I never said ten words to Harvey Tripp!"

"Nine was enough."

"Lila, my darling, we've been looking all over for you!" Czardi wedged himself between Lila and Norton and threw his arms around her and their cheeks brushed. "You look ravishingly exotic. You belong in Taj Mahal with a sultan at your feet." Norton wondered if Lila was wishing a magic carpet would materialize. "And Mr. Valentine. How nice to see you again. I don't believe you've met Burton Hartley." Hartley transferred his drink to his left hand and gave Norton a wet handshake.

"Glad to meet you, Mr. Hartley. I've been looking forward to it."

"I hear you bear sad tidings of Harvey Tripp. A most disagreeable person, Mr. Tripp. I can't believe he hung himself. Surely he died of satyriasis."

"No, he hung himself from a flagpole with a sashcord. Imported, of course."

"Tell them about his papers, Norton," interjected Lila shrewishly. "Or did Tripp omit fingering these boys?"

"Oh no, not at all. Sadly, gentlemen, you play minor parts in Harvey's treatise, but you're there all right."

"What is he talking about?" blustered Czardi as he began perspiring.

Hartley laughed and shook his head. "I've often wondered how this would end. Not with dignity, of course. There's never dignity in perfidy. I think the appropriate expression, Lila, is 'The jig's up.'" He moved back with amazing agility as she struck at the glass he was holding. "Temper! Temper! What a fiery creature she is, Mr. Valentine. Did you know we were once lovers? I even asked her to marry me, but now I'm glad she turned me down. She would have eaten our young."

"Shut your mouth, you drunken fool!" screeched Lila. "He doesn't have a damn thing on anybody. He's making it all up!"

"Hagar doesn't think so," said Hartley. "I think she's flown the coop. I saw her dashing up the grand staircase quite a few minutes ago, and I doubt if she was hurrying to her bathroom."

"I wonder why," mused Norton. "I never indicated to her she was mentioned."

"I don't think you had to. You told her his private papers indicated blackmail. Hagar is often given to a melodramatic turn of mind. Perhaps it's from all those potboilers she used to star in." He stood on his toes and scanned the room. "No, not a sign of her." He smiled at Lila. "Perhaps she's at the front door greeting guests. Or perhaps, Mr. Valentine, she's on the balcony of her boudoir scanning the rear of her grounds with her excellent pair of binoculars and seeing what I saw when I drove up along the back road." He now favored Lila. "I think the expression, Lila, is 'This castle is ringed.' Mr. Valentine, we all know you're with the secret service, and I am a coward. You see before you a friendly witness. The only fifths I take are bottled in bond."

Lila fled into the garden. "Lila!" shouted Czardi, "Lila, where are you going?"

Norton flagged a passing waiter carrying a tray of drinks and selected a scotch and water. He saw Hartley's Cheshire-cat grin. But he knew this time the smile would soon fade, and the cat would remain. "No pursuit, Mr. Valentine?"

"She won't get very far."

"As far as she needs to get, Mr. Valentine, which is the most convenient house telephone. The lesser two of Lila's necessary evils are hidden in my house. I believe they paid you a visit earlier this evening. Tom Gucci and Vince Hayes." Norton set his glass on a table. "But the remainder, a very large remainder, are scattered throughout Hagar's castle. They'll be troublesome. Whatever it is you're supposed to do, Mr. Valentine, I think you ought to do it."

"Mr. Hartley, I can't wait to find out why you decided to blow it for me."

"Oh, I've spent the whole day writing it, Mr. Valentine. It's all locked in my private safe. I made the futile gesture of resigning from an organization, an organization to which I have been of very minor use of late. But they don't like resignations. I only showed up tonight because I knew you'd be here. And I suspected you had every intention of rocking the boat. I'm asking for a lifesaver, Mr. Valentine."

"Thank you. I'll do the best I can." Norton strolled away and into the garden.

Czardi was mopping his brow. "They can't touch me. I have diplomatic immunity." Hartley snorted. From the garden, they heard two revolver shots.

Horace X. heard the police and ambulance sirens, and from around the curve ahead of him, he saw the reflection of headlights. His motorcycle was propped up against his thigh, and he held tightly to the handlebars, ready to straddle the seat, gun the motor, and deliver the tragic tidings of Viola's death to Chloe Jupiter. From behind him blended the additional sounds of a motorcycle and an automobile. He turned and saw the arrival of a motorcycle cop and Abe Grafton. As the cop and Grafton left their vehicles, the ambulance and police car pulled up. Boyd Gross struggled from behind the wheel as he saw Grafton reach Horace X., the black man, pointing to the ravine below. Grafton gestured over his shoulder to the motorcycle cop, who directed his headlight at the carnage below and then followed Grafton down the escarpment. Gross was questioning Horace X. when the ambulance attendants with a stretcher came hurrying to the road's edge.

"There's only one still alive," Horace X. shouted to the ambulance attendants. "She's about twenty feet past the convertible." He said to Gross, "Her passenger has a broken neck. Her name's Viola Fairbanks. She's Chloe Jupiter's niece."

"I know," said Gross. "Who are you?"

"Horace X.," said the black man, "Miss Jupiter's butler. The other car was a pickup truck. The driver's barbecued. I was out scouting for the ladies. They'd been overdue at Miss Jupiter's." He switched on his flashlight. "I saw these skid marks. There's a third set. The ladies were obviously forced off the road."

"You'd make a good detective, Horace." Gross surveyed the telltale tire marks with a grim expression. Horace X. was seated on his motorcycle gunning the engine.

"I have to tell Miss Jupiter," he explained to Gross.

"Get going." Gross waved him off. "I'll follow in a little while." Horace X. disappeared in a cloud of dust and exhaust fumes, as Gross hurried back to his car and contacted Ira Sparks at headquarters.

"He's not here," said the tense voice from the receiver. "We had the report of a rip-off at Hagar Simon's place. Sounds like all hell's broken loose out there." Gross rushed to the edge of the road, cupped his hands around his mouth, and shouted down to Grafton.

"Abe! *Abe!*"

The attendants were strapping the unconscious Marti Leigh to the stretcher. Grafton hallo'd acknowledgement to

Gross. "Take care of this!" shouted Gross. "There's a May Day at Hagar Simon's!"

Hagar Simon had changed into a black pantsuit and was opening her wall safe when she heard the revolver shots from the garden. She could feel the hairs rising on the nape of her neck as her face colored with apprehension. She worked the safe dial frantically and was oblivious to the sound of the door opening behind her. She pulled the safe door open and was reaching in to claim her treasures when Lila's rasping voice froze her. "Where the hell do you think *you're* going?"

Hagar spun around and saw Lila advancing on her menacingly. "I'm getting out. And don't you try to stop me." Her hand shot back into the safe like a greedy child given the run of a candy store. Lila lunged at her and dragged her away from the safe. Hagar's hand connected heavily with Lila's cheek. Lila bellowed in pain and outrage as she staggered back. Hagar rushed to her dressing table and tugged at the drawer containing the snub-nose automatic. Lila leapt on her back, her fingers clawing at Hagar's throat. Hagar gasped and sank to her knees, her hand now groping desperately on the tabletop for her heavy Louis XV hand mirror. Lila released one hand and grabbed for Hagar's wrist. Hagar heaved, and her body shot back like an angry mule's. Lila grunted and fell backwards. Hagar grabbed the hand mirror, staggered to Lila with the hand clutching the mirror upraised, and then struck her with brutal force on her left temple. Lila's eyes showed white as she went limp. Hagar fought for breath as she moved back against the dressing table. She could feel a thousand pinpricks as she clutched her breast. She doubled over, catching a glimpse of her unbecoming disarray in the dressing table mirror, and then edged her hand toward her bottle of nitroglycerine tablets. She thought of her handsome, muscular chauffeur and mewled pathetically. For the first time in years, she wished the late Isaac Simon was in the room with her to order a retake of the scene.

• • •

After firing the two revolver shots, Norton sprinted toward the rear of the castle. His bruised ligaments begged for mercy and admonished Norton, who cursed under his breath, as ahead of him loomed what appeared to be a deployment of adversaries. The moon appeared from behind a cloud, and the adversaries became a line of beautiful statues of Greek gods and goddesses, like a tableau of living statues he used to enjoy at the state fairs he attended in his childhood. He heard the crack of a pistol, and a bullet whistled over his head and blinded the eye of the goddess Aphrodite. He took cover behind Jupiter and saw at least a dozen men, some wearing waiter's jackets, converging toward him from the castle. From behind him he could hear the approach of other men and prayed it was his own associates. He heard the sound of gunfire from behind him, as the moon began to disappear behind another cloud. There were more bursts of gunfire, and he crouched lower behind Jupiter, his body aching mercilessly, his brows beaded with perspiration, blood pumping to his brain, alerting him to fulfill his most important mission, get Hagar Simon.

Inside the castle, the "Dance of the Hours" poured merrily from the loudspeakers. There was initially little panic among the guests. Hagar's bizarre entertainments were notorious, and old Margot piped a suggestion to her worried consort that perhaps a Wild West show was on the books for this evening. Burton Hartley went to a bar and helped himself to a stiffer drink, while Miklos Czardi, pushing his way through the guests to the front hall, looked as though he needed a wet suit.

On the grand staircase, several of Hagar's employees were working feverishly to dismantle the suits of armor where sophisticated microphones and high-powered cameras were hidden. Similar operations were being performed in the bedrooms and bathrooms. In the wine cellars and the basements, files were being emptied, and from the garage, the chauffeur was backing out a souped-up Volvo and wondering what the hell was keeping Hagar.

At the entrance to the estate, the sentries had been rounded up by several Feds and were being frisked, as a dozen other government men advanced on the castle.

From the heart-shaped balcony adjoining her boudoir, Chloe was watching the chaos at the castle through her pair of high-powered binoculars. In her bedroom, Irving the gorilla reluctantly left the television set and Bette Davis in *The Sisters* to join Chloe. In Chloe's garden and on her front lawn there was gathered a motley assortment of her retainers, former pugilists and wrestlers, dotted with a quartet of promising muscle men who inhabited the heart-shaped gymnasium and living quarters behind her pink house. Horace X. came roaring down the road and into the driveway. Chloe snapped her fingers at Irving the gorilla, and he followed her from the balcony into the bedroom and from there to her private heart-shaped elevator, which took them with dispatch to the floor below.

At the entrance to the castle, Ira Sparks arrived with two other squad cars, his eyes and face ablaze with anger at his authority being superseded. His loathing for Norton Valentine boiled at having been kept in ignorance of the planned federal raid.

In the blue salon of the castle, four people of apparent wealth and breeding were engrossedly engaged in a bridge game.

"Two no trumps!" blared East.

"Pass," said North glumly.

"Pass," said West sweetly, and East threw his cards in his wife's face.

In the grand hallway, Miklos Czardi held tightly to the arms of two women, trying desperately to camouflage himself between them as he guided them outside.

"But I don't want to leave!" cried one of the women, a blowsy blonde who slapped feebly at Czardi's hand.

On the upper landing, a man and woman were urging another struggling woman down the stairs.

"I won't go!" shrieked the woman, "I won't go without my husband!"

"Darling," said one of her would-be rescuers, "this is a raid; it's not the *Titanic!*"

Norton had abandoned Jupiter when he saw Hagar's gangsters dispersing at the sight of the federal agents swarming toward them from behind him. Norton reentered the castle through the kitchen and, waving his gun, demanded the location of the backstairs and got it from a terrified maid.

In Chloe Jupiter's sitting room, the dry-eyed woman handed her pink lace handkerchief to weeping Irving the Gorilla and addressed Horace X. and the assembly of her menials. Horace X.'s mother brought Chloe a heart-shaped glass of soda, which she sipped and then replaced on the tray Louella was holding. Chloe placed her hands on her hips and sternly addressed the assemblage.

"Gennulmen, muh niece Viola Fairbanks has been the victim of a vicious murderer. Uh want yuh tuh know, uh hold my'self tuh blame for it." She waved away the murmurs of dissent. Irving the Gorilla returned her handkerchief and was now crouched for action. "Uh been too smart for muh own good, and from muh binoculars, uh see Miss Simon's castle is bein' ripped off. Uh want Miss Simon delivered to me puhsonally. From heah on in, it's b'tween her and me. Horace X., uh want yuh tuh take Irvin' on yuh bike, and the rest of you boys go over in muh bus. Louella, bring me muh Bible and muh prayer shawl, and accompany me tuh muh private chapel."

Boyd Gross arrived at the castle and was waved through the gates by the government men. The area was jammed with automobiles, and he was forced to abandon his squad car and make his way to the castle on foot. From the castle wafted the strains of "The Lass with the Delicate Air." He passed Miklos Czardi futilely arguing with a federal agent. Inside the castle, Burton Hartley had found a telephone and was slurring a report on the bedlam to the night editor of his newspaper. The old juices were at a boil, and he felt young again. In this brief moment, he relived the triumphs of his youth as a callow reporter making his first scoop. This would be his last, and he treasured every moment of it. The night editor at the other end couldn't understand a word he was saying and was tearing at his sideburns with frustration.

The nitroglycerin tablets had revived Hagar to the extent that she was able to fill her jewel case hastily and pick her way past Lila Frank, lying prone on the floor, to a panel in the wall beyond her canopied bed. The panel was embossed with a fresco of Apollo, whose navel she pressed, and the wall panel slid back revealing a hidden passage. Lila groaned and began to revive. Her eyes fluttered open, and she felt her throbbing temple and the warm blood seeping from the wound. She struggled to her knees and saw Hagar disappear into the hidden passage and the panel slide shut behind her. "Putana!" gasped Lila, as she reached for a bed poster and pulled herself to her feet.

In the cavernous hallway outside, Norton was rushing from door to door in search of Hagar's bedroom. In some of the rooms, he saw Hagar's men tearing out fixtures and smashing false wall mirrors that revealed hidden rooms and cameras. Norton's own men were now converging, and he directed them toward their quarry. He rounded a corner and collided with Ira Sparks. Sparks's face contorted with recognition and hatred. Norton shouted, "Find Hagar Simon!" Sparks's gun hand shot out and connected with Norton's face. Norton staggered backward and caught himself from falling by grabbing the grillwork of an iron door that lead to one of the turrets. Sparks's foot shot out and caught Norton in the thigh. Norton lost his grip on the grillwork and fell to one knee. He shook his head to clear it, as Sparks's foot came toward him again. Norton dropped his revolver and grabbed Sparks's ankle and propelled the man on his back to the floor. "You're crazy, Ira!" shouted Norton. "You're crazy!" Sparks twisted his body with the amazing grace of a young athlete, and his fingers grabbed Norton by the hair. His beefy right fist shot up and struck Norton's face. Norton fell back against the grillwork door which gave way, and he landed on a concrete floor. He heard a voice shouting "Ira! For Christ's sake, Ira!" and recognized Boyd Gross. Madness and rage blinded Ira Sparks, and he leapt atop Norton. Norton jabbed him in the ribs, and Sparks fell to one side. Norton struggled to his feet, while Sparks pulled himself up, shifted his gun so that the handle was exposed, and delivered a powerful blow to Norton's skull. A beefy hand then took a grip on Norton's jacket and began pulling him up the stairs.

In the hallway, Boyd Gross collared a plainclothesman and shouted, "Come with me!"

Horace X.'s motorcycle came careening into the castle driveway. A federal man started to shout, "Halt!" but the word froze in his mouth at the sight of Irving the gorilla riding pillion, with his left hand gently holding Horace's waist, his right hand firmly clutching a pink truncheon. Behind Horace came the pink bus filled with the assorted pugs and athletes. Some of the once famous prizefighters were recognized, and shouts of greetings were exchanged.

Hagar's hidden passage led to a covered mall paved with flagstones that led to the garage. She shivered against the night air and the wind that was blowing up and could feel the dampness of the fog rolling in from the Pacific. She entered the garage by a side door and made her way past the Rolls Royce, the Cadillac, the Hispano-Suiza and the lawn mower. The high-powered Volvo was there, and the engine was running, and behind it the garage door was raised, but there was no sign of the chauffeur.

"Peter!" she shouted. "Peter, where are you?"

She looked inside the Volvo and saw her small suitcase and Peter's on the backseat. She checked and saw the car keys were in the ignition. She got in behind the wheel, placed the jewel box on the seat next to her, and started the motor. She backed out of the garage and then saw it was impossible to attempt to leave by the front gate. She reversed the car and nosed it around the garage to the small road leading to the back exit. She was seen by a federal man, who fired one shot over the Volvo. Horace X. at first thought the shot was directed at him and swerved the motorcycle almost dislodging Irving the Gorilla. Then he saw the Volvo disappearing behind the garage, and Irving jabbed him frantically. Irving recognized the Volvo. Horace X. gunned his motor and took off in hot pursuit.

In her private chapel, Chloe Jupiter, with her faithful housekeeper Louella, knelt on pink heart-shaped cushions and prayed. Candles were lit and sent flickering shadows across her sad, lovely face.

"Uh want yuh tuh have mercy on muh niece, Viola Fairbanks, who has come tuh yuh for the rest and peace she has earned. Viola was a good kid but had no mother tuh guide her. Her mother was a immoral puhson what got thrown outta Pittsburgh for corruptin' miners. But on her deathbed, uh promised tuh do muh best for Viola. Muh best wasn't good enough." Louella sobbed softly and shook her head from side to side. How often, until Chloe had discovered her son rioting on television, had she feared the possibility of mourning his death. Even now, while praying for the safekeeping of Viola's soul, her mind dwelled on the possible danger he faced at Hagar's castle. "Punish me as yuh see fit, Lord," continued Chloe, "but grant me one favor before yuh pernt yuh finger. Deliver into muh hands Hagar Holt Simon. Ahhhhhh-*men*."

Norton had been dragged by Sparks up the stone staircase

to the dizzying height of the rampart. Sparks breathed heavily as he struggled with the weight of Norton's body. As they reached the rampart, Norton began to revive. His head throbbed, his body ached, and he could faintly hear the scraping of heels, as he was being dragged along the flagstone floor. Sparks mustered his strength and heaved Norton to his feet, propping him against the edge of the stone parapet. The wind whistled around their ears, and the dampness of the fog brought a clamminess to their skins. Norton's eyes opened slowly, but they were slow to focus. Dimly he made out the form of a man, and he could feel a pressure on his chest forcing him back. He felt himself losing his balance and started to panic. "Oh!" he said. "Oh, Christ!" He felt a strong grip on his ankles, and now he realized he was teetering dangerously on the edge of the stone parapet. The danger revived his senses, and his arms began flailing wildly. He heard ugly laughter through heavy breathing and thought to himself:

Young man, I think you've had it.

11

Boyd Gross and the plainclothesman took the stone steps
leading to the rampart two at a time. Boyd was the first to
arrive at the top and saw Ira Sparks gripping Norton's ankles
and Norton's arms flailing helplessly. Behind him Gross
heard the plainclothesman ejaculate an astonished expletive,
and the two of them lunged at Sparks. Sparks released his
grip on Norton's ankles, and the hapless young man started
to fall. Gross left Sparks to the plainclothesman and leapt for
Norton, securing a good grip on his trouser waist and jacket.
Sparks fought like a wild animal, and his stunned opponent
was no match for him. He was too bewildered by the rush of
events. Had Sparks been trying to rescue the guy or kill him?
Sparks unleashed a powerful blow to his midriff that sent him
reeling against Gross. Gross let out a yell as he almost lost his
grip on Norton. Norton let out a yell as he felt himself
slipping again. And Sparks disappeared down the stone
steps. The plainclothesman got to his feet clutching his
midriff, while fleetingly entertaining the thought of demanding a transfer to another precinct, then responded to Gross's
cries for assistance. Together, they pulled Norton to safety.

Gross barked at his suffering assistant, "Get after Sparks . . . collar him . . . don't let him get away!"

Norton gasped, "Don't let him get near Hagar . . . Christ, don't let him get near her," and then sagged to his knees.

Lila Frank sat on the toilet seat of Hagar Simon's bathroom, holding a wet towel to her bleeding temple. Her sari was bloodstained, and she was missing one of her sandals. She could hear the shouts and cries coming from all points of the castle and disregarded them with an amazing, disciplinary inner aplomb, as she concentrated on easing the pain in her head and thinking of how to brazen her way out of this situation. She wondered if somewhere in Hagar's cavernous clothes closet she might find a black cape and a hat with a voluminous black veil. She wondered if she dared use Hagar's private line to phone Tom Gucci and Vince Hayes, sequestered at Burton Hartley's house. She envisioned them at Hartley's kitchen table swilling beer and playing gin rummy and silently invoked imprecations against both of them. She heard someone come thundering into the bedroom shouting, "Hagar! Hagar, you stinking bitch! *Hagar!*" and jumped to her feet like a startled gazelle. She saw a wild-eyed Ira Sparks brandishing his service revolver and, with a yelp of fear, slammed the door shut and fumbled with the lock.

Sparks leapt at the door and began beating at it with the butt of his gun. "Come out, Hagar! Come out of there!"

Lila Frank leaned against the door, frightened and confused. He's shouting *Hagar.* Not, "Come out, Mrs. Simon," or "Come out, lady. We got the goods on you."

Hagar, you stinking bitch!

Well, I'll be damned, thought Lila, well, I'll be good and damned. So *he's* what Hagar's been up to on the sly! A cop! A slimy fuzz . . . Ira Sparks!

Sparks' revolver exploded, and a bullet tore through the wooden frame of the bathroom door. Lila screamed and clutched her left hip. She sank to the tiles and dragged herself away from the door, whimpering. She heard a second shot from the bedroom and screamed.

In the bedroom, Sparks clutched his bleeding right shoulder, his revolver having fallen to the floor. The plainclothesman stood trembling in the doorway, his gun aimed at his superior. Boyd Gross and Norton arrived and pushed their way past the man. They heard Sparks say in an ugly voice to the plainclothesman, "McCarthy, I'm gonna bust you for this!"

Hagar Simon knew her heart couldn't take much more of this. She was zig-zagging the Volvo around the rear of the castle grounds, constantly cut off from the escape by Horace X.'s deft manipulations of his motorcycle. She crashed into a statue of a winged Mercury, amputating his outstretched leg and then ricocheted into and castrated the statue of Jupiter. The pink bus was parked at a safe distance waiting for the motorized game of cat and mouse to end. Most of the passengers had disembarked to see if they were needed inside the castle. Hagar cursed aloud the name of her defected paramour, the chauffeur.

The chauffeur was on the front lawn, strolling arm in arm with the agent whose full-length mirror at home reassured him daily he was every bit as beautiful as Mark Spitz. The chauffeur was telling the agent, "After I left the Pasadena Playhouse, I tested at Metro, and then I got the lead in a low budget porno movie called *Show It Hard*. Then I was up for this jockey-short commercial, but I lost it to a friend of the director, so you know how it is. I had to take this job chauffeuring for Mrs. Simon. Well, you know how it is with these oversexed old bags . . ."

"I most certainly do," sympathized the agent, as he clucked his tongue, disengaged his arm, and patted the chauffeur tenderly on his back side, "and I think you have the makings of a big, *big* star."

The plainclothesman, who had been sent by Boyd Gross to

find Abe Grafton, returned with him to Hagar's boudoir, where they saw Ira Sparks sitting up against the headboard of Hagar's bed, still trying to staunch the flow of blood from his right shoulder with his left hand. Boyd stared at Sparks with a look that was a mixture of pity and loathing. Norton was in the bathroom helping a protesting Lila Frank to her feet. Norton saw that Sparks's bullet had barely grazed her hip and tried to help her adjust her slipping sari, which was threatening to expose one of her breasts. Lila slapped his hands away.

"Where's Hagar?"

Lila tugged at the sari and said blisteringly, "She walked through the wall."

"Her safe's open. She's taken her valuables. Which way is she heading?"

"To hell, I hope. She'd better be, because when we catch up with her . . ." She caught herself, but too late.

Norton selected one word from her threatening tirade and repeated it blissfully. "We." Lila stared at herself in the mirror of the medicine chest and saw the ugly, blood-caked, bruised temple. She said weakly, "That was the editorial we."

"I think it was the organizational we, Lila. This operation is finished. You're finished. I'm still offering a deal."

The driver of the pink bus decided it was time to get into the act. He revved his motor and turned his wheel in the direction of the motorcycle and Volvo. Horace X. had tried again to cut across Hagar's path, and this time Irving the Gorilla lost his balance. He somersaulted backwards from his pillion position and landed on his feet in a crouch. Midway in the air he lost the pink truncheon. He snorted angrily and then looked up and saw the low-hanging branch of a tree. He leapt and caught the branch and then swung from tree to tree, craftily waiting for Hagar to drive by under him.

The pink bus was now pulling in across Hagar's path. She frantically applied her brakes, and Irving the Gorilla found his opportunity. He landed on the roof of the Volvo, crouched down, reached for the handle of the door on the passenger side, and wrenched it open. He nimbly swung himself over and into the car next to Hagar. He switched off the ignition, pulled out the keys, and flung them out the door. Then he folded his arms and glared at Hagar with a snarling severity. Hagar shrieked, clutched her heart, and fainted. Horace X. opened the door on her side, lifted Hagar in his arms, and carried her to the pink bus. Irving the Gorilla took Hagar's jewel case and followed Horace X. and his burden to the bus. Horace X. returned to his motorcycle, set it erect, climbed on, and gunned his motor. He led the way to the front gate and back to Chloe Jupiter's house.

By now, most of the innocent guests had been cleared and had departed, after giving their names and addresses. Burton Hartley and Miklos Czardi were among those detained, along with some two dozen hoodlums and gangsters rounded up by the secret service men and the police. Hartley and Czardi were on the front lawn, Czardi protesting vociferously and demanding the right to phone the Hungarian embassy. Hartley espied Horace X. on his motorcycle followed by the pink bus, in which he saw the limp Hagar nestling in the arms of Irving the Gorilla. He advised a secret service man to relay this information to Norton Valentine.

Ira Sparks was stoically silent as he was led down the stairs past the dismantled suits of armor. The once stately interior of the castle now looked as though it had been raped, stripped, and pillaged by hordes of invading Tartars. Lila Frank was being assisted down the grand stairway, limping with the lack of one sandal, clutching her hip where the bullet had grazed it, by a very impressed Abe Grafton. He couldn't wait to tell his wife and his girl friend that he had spent part of the evening with the celebrated columnist.

Norton was told that Hagar had been taken to Chloe Jupiter's house and looked exasperated. And then it suddenly came back to him. Marti and Viola! What had become of

Marti and Viola? He grabbed Boyd Gross's arm. "The girls! Marti Leigh and Viola Fairbanks! What happened to them? Where are they?" Boyd told him the little he knew. The girls had been forced off Malibu Canyon Road, crashed into a pickup truck. The driver of the truck was burnt to death, Viola's neck was broken, and she was dead, but at the time there seemed some hope of Marti's surviving. Norton glared at Ira Sparks, who met his gaze with uncompromising defiance and hatred. He held a sly smile of mockery, and Norton had to restrain himself from smashing a fist in his face. He turned back to Boyd Gross.

"Where would they have taken Marti?"

"Los Angeles General."

"Get somebody to check on her, will you? I want to take Sparks to Chloe Jupiter's. We'll bring Miss Frank with us." Lila was staring past him at Burton Hartley. Hartley searched her face for some sign of sympathy or understanding, but saw nothing but condemnation. "Boyd," said Norton, "if Marti's regained consciousness, find out what statement she's made. Maybe she recognized whoever forced them off the road." Boyd relayed the instructions to McCarthy, the plainclothesman, and McCarthy headed back into the castle at a trot.

Czardi and Hartley were led away into custody, while Norton crossed to a group of his own men and conferred briefly. The raid had been more successful than expected. They had luckily timed it right. Had they waited another day, the castle would have been stripped of microphones and cameras and incriminating files on over hundreds of newsworthy personalities. Nobody was elated. It was a depressing experience. The reverberations from this night's haul would be felt across not only the nation but the entire world, which would now have to face a serious devaluation of reputations. Norton requested two cars and an escort. Sparks and Lila were taken to separate cars, where they sat lost in their respective thoughts, while Norton and Boyd Gross awaited McCarthy's information from the hospital.

"You look as though you could use a doctor yourself," Gross said to Norton.

"I'll be okay," replied Norton, as he saw McCarthy hurrying toward them.

Earlier, while Norton had been offering Lila another chance at a deal, Marti Leigh lay in a state of semidelirium in a private room of the hospital. Outside in the corridor, a policeman guarded the door to her room. In Marti's room, a handsome young intern and a placid black nurse adjusted the weights that held her plaster-casted legs suspended from canvas-bottomed pulleys. Her face and both her hands were heavily bandaged. Detective Hank Rosen had been called back to duty and now anxiously waited for Marti to regain consciousness and give him a statement.

"The sky is falling, the sky is falling," mumbled Marti. Rosen didn't think it was worth making a note of that.

"Nortie . . . hurry, Nortie," continued Marti, and Rosen glanced at the intern, who shrugged.

"What's her chances?" Rosen asked the intern.

"It's anybody's guess," said the intern glumly. "I've seen some pull out of worse than this. I've seen others succumb to a simple fracture. It's the shock that does it."

"Shocking . . . very shocking," mumbled Marti.

Rosen turned to the nurse. "Say something to her."

"Like what?"

"I don't know. Anything. We've got to try to bring her around."

"Let me try," said the intern. He bent over Marti and spoke gently, "Miss Leigh . . . Miss Leigh . . . you're safe. You're alive. You're in the hospital, and you're being taken care of. Do you hear me, Miss Leigh?"

"Ummmm." Marti licked her lips and then groaned.

"Miss Leigh . . . this is Doctor Frisby . . . Lawrence Frisby . . ."

Marti groaned again and then slowly her eyes began to

open. It's the Fourth of July, she thought. It must be the Fourth of July. I can see a Catherine wheel spinning, and the rockets are bursting into crazy patterns of orange and purple and black. I'm eight years old, and if I let that man touch me where he wants to touch me, he'll buy me some spun sugar and maybe a hot dog, and if I play hard to get like Susie Schweiber taught me, maybe he'll take me on the carousel. "Wheeeee!" said Marti. The handsome young intern's face was coming into focus, and she blinked her eyes. She could see the intern's face clearly now, and it pleased her enormously.

"Hi there," she whispered, "what are you doing New Year's Eve?"

McCarthy came huffing and puffing back to Norton and Boyd Gross. "She's okay," said McCarthy, and Norton's face flooded with relief. "She was chased by some guy in a red Toyota. She couldn't see his face. It was hidden by a hat . . ." He continued talking, while Norton thought hard.

"A red Toyota." Norton snapped his fingers. "Karen Frost's car is that color and make."

"There are lots of them around," said Gross.

"Send somebody to the garage at Karen's place. Check if her car's still there, and if it is, I'll give you odds there'll be telltale marks on the right fender."

"If he used her car," mused Gross. "How cute can you get." He gave McCarthy the assignment.

"Let's get going," Norton said to Gross. The searching look on Gross's face held him. "What's bothering you?"

"Ira. I can't believe that . . . resentment . . . jealousy . . ." he was floundering for words, ". . . whatever the hell you want to call it . . . would drive him to trying to murder you."

Norton put his arm around Gross and guided him toward the squad car in which Ira Sparks sat in the back seat between two detectives. "Boyd, old buddy, I'm too tired and in too much pain to give you a lecture on your favorite subject. But when we get to Chloe Jupiter's, I think it'll all come out in the wash. Back there in Hagar's suite, that wasn't Lila Frank he thought he was shooting at. He was gunning for Hagar Simon. I think you can take it from there, if you start working backward."

"Ira's shoulder should be attended to."

"I don't give a damn if he bleeds to death! I hate that animal. He's not good enough to be called *pig*." Norton had wrenched open the door to the squad car and was staring directly at Ira Sparks. He was chagrined to see the man was in tears.

Burton Hartley was working overtime, currying favor with the detectives in the squad car transporting him and Miklos Czardi to central headquarters. Czardi was wondering how much he might get for his life story from *Esquire* if he got May Mann to ghost it. Hartley was telling the officers where to find Tom Gucci and Vince Hayes. There was a beatific expression on his face as he spoke. Burton Hartley felt he had found peace at last.

Back at the castle in the wreckage of the grounds at the rear, the septuagenarian Margot was leading her young Latin lover Manuel along a path strewn with shattered pieces of statuary and broken turf. She held tightly to his arm as she looked around her, like a dowager empress examining the ruins of a fallen empire. "You'll never see the likes of this again, Manuel," she cackled. "It's the last dinosaur. I caught that sly glance, you wicked thing. I'm the last pterodactyl. But all this," she waved a feeble hand in the direction of the castle, "will soon be razed and carted away. It was the last majestic symbol of old Hollywood. They'll subdivide this land and build dreadful little ranch type houses and destroy every trace of dear Isaac Simon's dream. Poor Isaac. Another Pygmalion destroyed by his Galatea. Did I ever tell you he was my first lover?" Manuel shook his head no as he stared at the castle and shivered. It was enshrouded with fog, and in the hazy glow of moonlight, he expected the frightening shade of a vampire to materialize on one of the ramparts.

"Isaac was a gentle man and a loving man, and this castle should be preserved as his monument. But nowadays we trade our monuments for oil wells and supermarkets. Put your arm around me, Manuel. I'm cold. I'm very cold. Let's go to Gatsby's."

Hagar Simon was stretched across the ermine-covered couch of Chloe Jupiter's reception room. Her hands were folded across her chest, and her skin held a ghostly pallor. Chloe stared down at the unconscious woman, tapping her foot impatiently, hands on her hips, jewels sparkling on the fingers of her hands. She tossed her lavish red mane and quipped, "Mebbe uh oughta put a lily between her fingers. Louella, Horace X, get tuh work on her wrists." She peered closely at Hagar's face. "Mebbe we oughta hold a mirror to her nose."

Irving the Gorilla was rummaging through Hagar's jewel box and found the bottle of nitroglycerin tablets. He had already frisked her purse and given her snub-nosed revolver to Horace X. for safekeeping. He waddled over to Chloe and gave her the bottle. Chloe red the label and commented, "So, she's still got a heart. Here, Louella, open this thing and shove some of them pills into her mouth. Then wipe all the fingerprints from the bottle." She circled the sofa and went to Horace X., who was massaging Hagar's left wrist. "Horace X., yuh give the undertaker full instructions for Viola's funeral?" Horace X. nodded. "Good. Uh'll speak tuh Liberace puhsonally about the music uh want played, and uh'll work up a new arrangement of 'Lover' for Peggy Lee tuh sing."

Louella had forced two pills between Hagar's lips and was gently massaging her throat. Chloe strolled past her with impatience and said to Louella, "Uh'd sooner see yuh usin' a knife exceptin' uh want her tuh heah me speak muh piece. Uh tell yuh, it'll take a year of Hail Mary's and novenas before uh'm forgiven for muh sins of omission. Uh shoulda known the party was over when Norton came around tuh see me. Uh shoulda spilled the works 'n' saved Viola's life."

Horace X. said, "You couldn't have foreseen any of this."

"Uh know uh couldn't!" stormed Chloe. "Uh shoulda had the sense tuh consult Carroll Righter."

Irving the Gorilla heard the squad cars coming up the drive and set up a racket. Chloe sauntered to a front window and pulled back the ermine drapes. She saw Norton and the other detectives pouring out of the two cars with Ira Sparks and Lila Frank. "Ummmmm," murmured Chloe eyeing the detectives, "fresh men." She left the window and sauntered back to the sofa. "Horace X., we got uninvited company. Yuh better let 'em in. Uh don't mind an audience when uh tell Hagar what uh think of her."

"She's coming to," said Louella.

"Tuh what?" snapped Chloe. Irving the Gorilla was jumping up and down and chattering with excitement. "Irvin'! Settle down 'n' stop behavin' like uh ape." Irving the Gorilla slunk to the bar, hoisted himself on an ermine covered stool, and crossed his legs. He found a swizzle stick and rolled it back and forth between thumb and index finger. "That's better, Irvin'," said Chloe. "Yuh look suave. Yuh look like the late Adolphe Menjou."

Norton entered followed by Boyd Gross. Two detectives had a tight grip on each of Ira Sparks' arms, and he was wincing with pain. Lila Frank entered between another pair of detectives, one hand on her bruised hip.

Chloe glowered at Lila. "Yuh tryin' tuh imitate me, Lila?"

"No," growled Lila, "I got shot in the ass."

"Ummmm . . . uh'm shuah it ain't the first time. Hullo, Norton, yuh look like yuh been in a cement mixer. Horace X., uh think these gents could use a drink." She watched Ira Sparks lower himself onto a chair. She asked Norton, "What's with the detective man, Norton? He looks more like a prisoner."

Norton was staring at Hagar, watching the color come back

to her face. "Among other things, he tried to murder me tonight."

"Well, that certainly wasn't very Christian of him." Lila sat in an easy chair across from the sofa, staring stonily at Hagar. Chloe moved toward her with undulating hips. "Uh told yuh a long time ago they'd catch up with yuh sooner or later, Lila. Yuh shoulda took muh advice and gone tuh live in Italy."

"Up you!"

"Vulgarity ain't no fit substitute for wit." She smiled at Norton. "Uh think that's Voltaire. If it ain't, then it's mine. Uh suppose uh had no right abductin' Hagar the way uh did, Norton, but uh wanted a private confrontation befoah turnin' her over tuh yuh. Well, uh learned a long time ago ah can't have everythin'." She sighed and added, "Uh suppose havin' everyone is enough compensation. Norton, uh'm invitin' yuh to Viola's funeral. Uh hope yuh can come. Uh'm flyin' in Lenny Bernstein tuh conduct *The Messiah.* 'N' that's just for openers." She began to take full advantage of her unexpected audience and paraded about the room with a variety of her timeworn and familiar gestures. "Uh want this tuh be a gay occasion. Uh don't want no tears. Uh want laughter because my niece always enjoyed a good time. Sayyyyy! How's the other kid? How's Marti Leigh?"

"She might pull through," said Norton. He was watching Louella helping a groggy Hagar to sit up.

"Yuh don't sound so hot tuh me, Norton. Yuh sound worse than yuh look. What's eatin' yuh?"

Norton took a heart-shaped glass of scotch and water from Horace X. "Marti Leigh's my former wife." He heard an intake of breath and decided it came from Lila. Hagar was staring about the room in bewilderment and then saw Ira Sparks. She whimpered pitifully, and Louella patted her gently on the back.

"Yuh still torchin' for Miss Leigh, Norton?"

Norton got to his feet. "I've more important things to attend to now, Chloe. Do you have a tape recorder?"

"Why, shuah, uh have a tape recorder. Muh place is

equipped with every modern convenience exceptin' compu-
ters. Irvin'! Go tuh muh room 'n' get muh heart-shaped tape
recorder." She said over her shoulder to Norton, "Uh had it
made especially for me in Japan." She looked at Ira Sparks's
injured shoulder. "Louella, uh think the detective man over
theah could use some first aid. Yuh can apply yuh second aid
to Miss Frank's left rear bumper."

Irving the gorilla returned with the tape recorder, and
Boyd Gross set it up on the heart-shaped coffee table.
"There's a fresh long-playin' tape in it," Chloe told Norton.
"Uh was gonna rehearse muh lines for a show uh'm gonna do
in Chicago. It's called *Mother Courage*."

Norton found a smile at last. "You're going to do Brecht?"

"No, he'd dead. Uh'm just gonna do his play. Uh'm gettin'
the Sondheim kid tuh write me some songs, 'n' of course uh'll
be playin' the thing for laughs." She smiled at Boyd Gross.
"Uh see yuh got mechanical fingers. Norton, since uh'm the
star of this place, uh always get top billin'. So uh'm gonna
begin and speak muh piece first. Horace X., give Hagar
Simon some spirits tuh sip on." She smiled at Hagar with
irony. "Yuh lucky uh don't stock hemlock."

"I'm not well," muttered Hagar weakly, "I'm not well. I
must have a doctor. My heart . . . please understand . . .
I've had three attacks today . . . please somebody . . .
please . . ."

Boyd instructed one of the detectives to phone for an
ambulance. Chloe started the tape recorder.

"This begins a long time ago, Norton, long befoah a lot of
yuh was born. But it helps explain the events leadin' up tuh
the tragedies. Irvin', bring me a glass of muh mineral water."
She folded her arms and began pacing back and forth. She
saw an anxious look on Norton's face. "Don't worry about
muh walkin' back 'n' forth. This tape recorder picks up yuh
voice from a hundred yards or more. It's like the stuff Hagar
got placed all over the castle. Uh'm shuah you found them.
Well, Norton, uh'm shuah yuh heard of Salvatore Gucci, 'n'
so yuh heard of his eldest son Cristo."

"Chloe!"

"Shut up, Lila, this is muh big scene." Irving the gorilla gave Chloe the mineral water, and she sipped it delicately. "Well, a long time ago, Norton, when I was tryin' tuh crack intuh the movies, uh met Cristo. We fell for each other, and we fell hard. Uh'd been havin' talks with the late Isaac Simon about coproducin' with him some pictures independently, but we were both short of bread. That's where Cristo comes in. He gets the money from his old man, Salvatore. Shortly after this, yuh know, you boys got the goods on Salvatore and kicked him outta the country.

"Well, by this time, Isaac 'n' I have finished our first fillum, 'n' it's a smash hit. It puts Isaac right on top with the big boys, 'n' we got one smash hit after another. Meantime, Cristo 'n' I are driftin' apart because he's taken over his father's empire, 'n' as y' can well imagine, that requires a lot of . . . ummmmm . . . paperwork. Cristo's in New York, and I'm heah in the West, 'n' yuh know y'can't hold a romance together by mailin' it t'each other. But Cristo 'n' I stays friends. The family has a big investment in me.

"Well, all this time, old Salvatore is champin' tuh get back into the states. 'N' tuh do that he needs power . . . power over the people who could get the papers signed that'd let him back in. So he comes up with this scheme, which he's seen operatin' profitably in London 'n' in Rome. Well, of course, it's takin' a long time tuh get this scheme operatin', 'n' by this time poor old Isaac is head over heels infatchewated with Hagar heah 'n' losin' his money promotin' her into a star. He's sellin' everythin', includin' the castle.

"Norton, uh own that castle."

Lila Frank started to jump from her seat, but Irving the Gorilla pulled her back from behind. She sent a stream of invective in his direction, and he mockingly covered his ears. Boyd Gross sharply ordered her to belt up.

"Yah, Norton, that's all muh property yuh been wreckin' t'night. Long about the time I took title tuh the castle, Cristo sends me an emissary with his proposition. I should move into the castle and do the job for him Hagar's been doin'. Well y'know, Norton, uh'm a very loyal person. B'cause of muh religious beliefs, uh don't hold with nothin' immoral, illegal or illicit. But I owe the Gucci family. They put me where uh am t'day. Uh tell 'em they can have the castle, but they'll have tuh put someone else in tuh run it for them.

"Well, by this time, Gucci has quietly bought in tuh television 'n' radio 'n' films 'n' yeah, newspapers and some big newspaper syndicates. They need someone they can trust out here, so they create a celebrity. Right, Lila?"

Lila was staring at Chloe, while playing pat-a-cake with her fingers. "You tell it the way you know it, Chloe," said Lila huskily with a trace of venom. "This is your big scene. Make the most of it. It'll be your last."

Chloe replied icily, "Uh would'n' give yuh odds on that threat. Well, anyway, Norton, it's right about this time uh read that Cristo's been murdered on his own front lawn. Half his head shot away. Uh'll tell yuh why. He didn't want the old man back here. The old man's gettin' senile. He's crazy."

"He's not!" Irving the Gorilla pulled Lila back into the chair.

"It's like a Greek tragedy what happened tuh Cristo. His own kids, his own flesh 'n' blood, schemed tuh erase him. Because old Salvatore promised them power and money. He said he'd make 'em bigger than royalty. So Cristo's own son kills him and then comes West where his sister looks after him."

She paused dramatically and sauntered over to Lila. "The son what did the killin' is Tom Gucci. His sister is sittin' right here. Camille Gucci."

"Putana!"

"Whatever that is, honey, don't use too much garlic. So anyway, there's Hagar over here scratchin' at muh door back then, askin' for help. So uh turns her over to Camille or Lila or whatever yuh wanna call her. She's the bag woman for the old man."

Norton said to Lila, "Which explains the trips to Europe."

Lila threw her head back and stared at the ceiling. The cherubs painted there seemed to look down on her with disapproval. Then she sat up, looking directly at Norton. "Okay, Mr. Valentine, I'll take that deal."

Norton stirred the ice cubes in his glass with an index finger. "The offer's rescinded, Lila."

Lila said with a smirk, "Indian giver." Irving the Gorilla made a move to swat the back of her head, but his hand was arrested by a stern look from Chloe.

Chloe recaptured center stage. "Uh'd a kept muh mouth shut, Norton, but like uh told yuh this mornin', uh don't hold with murder. In case yuh don't know, Lila, uh'm who told Norton Clay Stopley was at Hagar's Monday night."

Lila was staring at Hagar with blazing hatred. Hagar was staring across the room at Ira Sparks. Slowly she raised her hand and pointed a finger at him.

"There's your murderer. There's the damn fool who killed Clay Stopley. One of your finest. One of your best. Ira Sparks. My lover."

12

Ira Sparks removed his jacket. Louella had cut away his shirt with a scissors and was applying medication to his bullet wound. Now he brusquely shoved her away and leaned forward with his hands clutching his knees. "You were running away without me, Hagar. Why were you running away without me?"

Norton didn't recognize his voice. It was small and weak and sounded like the mock imitation of a child. For a wild moment Norton looked around the room to see if anyone was a ventriloquist throwing their voice.

"Why, Hagar? *Why?*"

Hagar pulled herself to a sitting position. "Because I loathed you. I loathed your touch, your slobbering kisses, your pathetic attempts at masculinity in the bedroom."

It took two men to restrain Sparks. He shrieked and cursed and then embarrassed them all by breaking into infantile sobs. Hagar's voice rose above the cacophony he was creating, as she looked directly at Norton.

"And I hated him for murdering Clay Stopley. My deal promised me no murder! I said that to him up on the rampart, as he grabbed that bewildered young man by the ankles and sent him plunging to his death. *Not murder!* Ira is such a fool, such a desperate fool. He'd heard I'd been having an affair with my chauffeur."

Lila guffawed.

Hagar turned to her with a sulfuric look. "Peter's more of a man than your pathetic Burton Hartley."

"Ah, that was finished long ago." Lila sat with one hand dangling over the arm of her chair.

"I'd like to hear the rest of this, Hagar."

Hagar smiled at Norton. "Of course, you would. And so you shall. He chose Monday night to come to the castle and confront me. Your Mr. Stopley had been fed some fly agaric in his mushroom soup. Not too much, just enough to dull his senses. We weren't sure if he was a secret service man or not. But Burton was suspicious of some of his more leading questions and urged an ounce of prevention. So it was slipped into his soup. Karen knew what was happening, and she misbehaved badly to me. She was in love with Stopley. And I suspected she knew the truth of his identity. But we were interrupted by my maid. She told me Ira was in my bedroom. He slips in and out when he wants to because there's an old secret passage leading there. I used it to try and get away this evening."

"I told you she walked through the wall, Norton," said Lila wryly. "You can't say I haven't been honest with you at least once this evening."

"I thank you for the small favor. And for my beating."

"That was their own idea!"

"Shall I continue, Norton?" chirruped Hagar.

"I'd be very grateful."

"Thank you. I went to the bedroom, and there was an ugly scene with Ira. Clay Stopley was apparently stumbling around the house. He overheard us and poked his head in the door. We should have given him a heavier dose, because he recognized Ira. Well, I'm sure you know what kind of a rampaging bull Ira can turn into. He went after Stopley and began beating him mercilessly. I tried to pull Ira away, and Mr. Stopley fled up the stairs to the rampart. Ira pushed me aside . . . *quite* brutally, I might add . . . and chased him up there. I followed. I saw Ira kill him. With the help of some of my men, Ira took the body to Griffith Park. Ira will have to tell you the rest. I only know what I read in the papers."

Sparks had calmed down and was blowing his nose in his bandanna handkerchief. Irving the Gorilla regarded him with distaste.

"I hate your guts, Mr. Valentine."

"I know that, Ira."

"I hated Stopley for ignoring me the way he did. And I hated you for going out of your way to make me feel needed. You think I didn't know you had more respect for this shit!" He gestured toward Boyd Gross, who stared at the floor. "Hagar and me were going away together. She promised me that. I got a desk drawer filled with travel folders. We were lovers before she married Simon. When I was still a cop assigned to guard the stage door entrance at the arena. I mean . . ." his hands were outstretched with bewilderment, ". . . for years I stuck by her. I gave her money when she was broke. Then when she told me about fronting for the Gucci bunch and that, when she had her new pile made, we'd go away together . . . make a life together . . . I . . . I . . ."

"Sold yourself for a mess of pottage."

Sparks's eyes narrowed. "Well, why not, Mr. Valentine? Why not? It's a better reward than a gold watch and a slap on the back and a crappy pension that wouldn't feed a cage full of pigeons." He stared at his hands as though they were a surprise gift and then let them dangle as he slumped in his chair. "I was dumb. I was very dumb. I should have tossed Stopley's body in the drink for the fish to feast on. But I was in a panic, I guess. So I stripped his pockets and bashed his face in with a rock and took the rock and his wallet and everything else I found back to my apartment. Then I remembered Karen Frost. Hagar had told me she was in love with Stopley. I went to her apartment. I parked in the garage, and her car was there. I was using my own car. Nobody would guess it was a cop's. I went up to her place, and she wouldn't let me in at first. So I told her through the door that Stopley was okay. He was asking for her.

"She let me in. I grabbed her by the neck and warned her, if she said anything about Stopley, I'd kill her. And that was my second mistake." His voice lowered. "She didn't even know who I was. She wouldn't have known I had been at Hagar's that night. Nobody knew I was mixed up with Hagar. I guess you've got it over me at that, Mr. Valentine. You'd of thought it out more. So I beat up on her, punched her in the eye. Made up a wild story that a lot of us cops were in on the deal. That she'd better shut up, or she'd get it next.

"Then the next day, I went through the motions of interviewing some of the guests. And then you came to town, Mr. Valentine. And you frightened the hell out of me. I wanted Hagar and me to skip that night. But Hagar was stalling. She had sworn the chauffeur was nothing to her. She has a way of making me believe things."

Hagar was massaging the area around her heart and looking properly modest. In the distance Norton heard the sound of the approaching police ambulance. He said to Sparks, "You killed Karen shortly after I left your office with Boyd." Sparks nodded. "You delayed putting a guard on her until after murdering her. You took her diary, her appointment book . . ."

"I took everything I could lay my hands on. And then I read in her handwriting she'd been visited by you, Marti Leigh and Viola Fairbanks. It was too late to turn back then. I had to get rid of both those broads."

"Yuh monster." Chloe drew Louella away from him, as though Sparks might be infectious.

"I made up this cock-and-bull about seeing my doctor. I'm a diabetic."

"I know that," said Norton. "You used your own syringe to plunge the air bubble into her vein."

"Yeah. Then I forced the dissolved sleeping pills into her mouth while she was gasping for air."

Chloe crossed herself. "Even now uh'm askin' God tuh show yuh some mercy. If it was up tuh me, uh wouldn't."

Norton waved her to be quiet. "Tell us how you went after the girls."

"I went after Marti Leigh. I didn't know the Fairbanks kid would be with her." He said with irony, "Some days even I run lucky. I didn't want to use my own car. In case I slipped up, my license plates might be seen and traced. I had the keys to Frost's red Toyota." Norton couldn't resist an I-told-you-so look at Boyd Gross. Gross looked as though he had just heard a filthy epithet directed at the Pope. He was listening to Ira Sparks with dismay, disgust and disappointment. He was thinking of this black mark against his department.

"I parked my car a block away from Frost's place and took her car and drove out to Malibu. I got there just as I saw Leigh and the Fairbanks kid driving off in Leigh's yellow Chrysler convertible. Do I have to tell you the rest? I forced them off the road. I killed them."

"Marti Leigh's still alive," Norton said with some difficulty. "When Boyd heard you making the all-points alert for the girls, he thought he heard you mentioning the make and color of the car."

"Yeah, I started to. Then I caught myself. Just once I used my effing brains! Just that once!"

The police ambulance had arrived, and Horace X. went to the door. The phone rang, and Louella answered it. "Mr. Boyd Gross?" Gross crossed to her and took the phone. It was McCarthy on the other end. "Thanks, McCarthy. Norton guessed right on the Toyota." Norton tried not to look as though a laurel wreath had been placed on his head. "What was that, McCarthy?" Gross had a look of surprise. "Well, that's a pleasant bonus. Hey, Norton. The boys have rounded up Gucci and Hayes." Lila whispered a four-letter word. "They were tipped by our new friend Burton Hartley. He had them stashed at his place." Lila added to the variety of her gutter vocabulary with another four-letter word. "Okay, McCarthy. See you soon."

The ambulance attendants entered with a stretcher but couldn't see a victim.

"It's for Mrs. Simon over heah on muh sofa," said Chloe. "She's expectin' a heart attack."

"Chloe." Hagar sat forward. "Believe me, Chloe, please believe me, I swear it on Isaac's soul . . . I'd have sacrificed myself rather than see Viola dead."

Chloe looked at her with contempt. "Well, don't put it in writin'."

Boyd Gross was extracting the tape from the recorder. He had been given orders to have Sparks and Lila taken to central headquarters and booked. He would accompany Hagar in the ambulance. Norton asked Horace X. to take him back to the castle so he could pick up his Renault.

As the room began to empty, Chloe sauntered over to Norton and placed a hand on his shoulder. "Uh suppose yuh thinkin' of maybe reservin' a cell fuh me." Irving the Gorilla snorted and made his way to Chloe's side.

"You'll be subpoena'd, Chloe. But you've got powerful friends in the government." Norton winked at her.

"Ummmmm . . . uh've already got a call in to Louis Nizer, just in case." Norton took her in his arms and kissed her. "Ummmm . . . with a little more practice, Norton, yuh could enter the Olympics."

An hour later, Norton sat at Marti Leigh's bedside. He had tried without success to disguise his emotion at the sight of her when he entered her room. Though she was under sedation, she was still awake and although her face was heavily bandaged, obscuring her features, he sensed she was glad to see him. He placed his hand over her fingertips, and she responded lightly.

"All wrapped up?" she asked in a weak voice.

"You or the job?"

"Both."

"All wrapped up."

"Tell me about it. Fast. I feel myself slipping away."

He recapped the evening's events for her swiftly. She had no special reaction when he named Ira Sparks as the murderer. She merely said, "The son of a bitch."

"Let's leave him to heaven."

"That's not where he's going."

And she was asleep. Norton left the room. He returned to the hotel, opened the sliding doors to the swimming pool, and then mixed himself a drink. He dialed his office on the turquoise phone and spent almost an hour reciting a meticulously detailed report. He was surprised he didn't fall asleep in the middle of it. After he hung up, he stripped off what was left of his clothes and took a hot shower. After toweling himself and putting on a robe, he returned to the living room and found Boyd Gross sitting with a drink in his hand.

"I hope I didn't frighten the hell out of you," said Gross. "I came out to the pool to see if there was a light on in your room. I saw the doors were open. If you're too tired to talk, I'll go away. But I won't sleep a wink tonight. I won't sleep any, thinking about Ira."

"Sure, old buddy. I'm not in the least bit tired," he lied. He poured himself a fresh drink and then sat opposite Gross. Norton had wanted to talk all night, too. He wanted to talk to Marti and ask her to marry him again. He had wanted to talk to her about perhaps leaving the service and going away together to start a new life. But he also knew it was a pipe dream. He knew he wouldn't quit his job, and he knew Marti would reject him. He had thought it out driving back from Hagar's castle after picking up the Renault. He sat watching Boyd Gross staring out at the pool, probably trying to find the words he wanted to say or a reason for saying them. He settled back in his seat and waited.